OPENINGS IN THE OLD TRAIL

BRET HARTE

1st WORLD
LIBRARY
Literary Society

Openings in the Old Trail

Bret Harte

© 1st World Library, 2008
PO Box 2211
Fairfield, IA 52556
www.1stworldlibrary.com
First Edition

LCCN: 2007940175

Softcover ISBN: 978-1-4218-9312-9
Hardcover ISBN: 978-1-4218-9412-6
eBook ISBN: 978-1-4218-9212-2

Purchase *"Openings in the Old Trail"*
as a traditional bound book at:
www.1stWorldLibrary.com/purchase.asp?ISBN=978-1-4218-9312-9

1st World Library is a literary, educational organization
dedicated to:

- Creating a free internet library of downloadable ebooks

- Hosting writing competitions and offering book publishing
  scholarships.

Interested in more 1st World Library books? contact:
literacy@1stworldlibrary.com
Check us out at: www.1stworldlibrary.com

1St World Library Literary Society

Giving Back to the World

"If you want to work on the core problem, it's early school literacy."

- James Barksdale, former CEO of Netscape

"No skill is more crucial to the future of a child, or to a democratic and prosperous society, than literacy."

- Los Angeles Times

"Literacy... means far more than learning how to read and write... The aim is to transmit... knowledge and promote social participation."

- UNESCO

"Literacy is not a luxury, it is a right and a responsibility. If our world is to meet the challenges of the twenty-first century we must harness the energy and creativity of all our citizens."

- President Bill Clinton

"Parents should be encouraged to read to their children, and teachers should be equipped with all available techniques for teaching literacy, so the varying needs and capacities of individual kids can be taken into account."

- Hugh Mackay

CONTENTS

A MERCURY OF THE FOOT-HILLS

It was high hot noon on the Casket Ridge. Its very scant shade was restricted to a few dwarf Scotch firs, and was so perpendicularly cast that Leonidas Boone, seeking shelter from the heat, was obliged to draw himself up under one of them, as if it were an umbrella. Occasionally, with a boy's perversity, he permitted one bared foot to protrude beyond the sharply marked shadow until the burning sun forced him to draw it in again with a thrill of satisfaction. There was no earthly reason why he had not sought the larger shadows of the pine-trees which reared themselves against the Ridge on the slope below him, except that he was a boy, and perhaps even more superstitious and opinionated than most boys. Having got under this tree with infinite care, he had made up his mind that he would not move from it until its line of shade reached and touched a certain stone on the trail near him! WHY he did this he did not know, but he clung to his sublime purpose with the courage and tenacity of a youthful Casabianca. He was cramped, tickled by dust and fir sprays; he was supremely uncomfortable—but he stayed! A woodpecker was monotonously tapping in an adjacent pine, with measured intervals of silence, which he always firmly believed was a certain telegraphy of the bird's own making; a green-and-gold lizard flashed by his foot to stiffen itself suddenly with a rigidity equal to his own. Still HE stirred not. The shadow gradually crept nearer the mystic stone—

and touched it. He sprang up, shook himself, and prepared to go about his business. This was simply an errand to the post-office at the cross-roads, scarcely a mile from his father's house. He was already halfway there. He had taken only the better part of one hour for this desultory journey!

However, he now proceeded on his way, diverging only to follow a fresh rabbit-track a few hundred yards, to note that the animal had doubled twice against the wind, and then, naturally, he was obliged to look closely for other tracks to determine its pursuers. He paused also, but only for a moment, to rap thrice on the trunk of the pine where the woodpecker was at work, which he knew would make it cease work for a time—as it did. Having thus renewed his relations with nature, he discovered that one of the letters he was taking to the post-office had slipped in some mysterious way from the bosom of his shirt, where he carried them, past his waist-band into his trouser-leg, and was about to make a casual delivery of itself on the trail. This caused him to take out his letters and count them, when he found one missing. He had been given four letters to post—he had only three. There was a big one in his father's handwriting, two indistinctive ones of his mother's, and a smaller one of his sister's—THAT was gone! Not at all disconcerted, he calmly retraced his steps, following his own tracks minutely, with a grim face and a distinct delight in the process, while looking—perfunctorily—for the letter. In the midst of this slow progress a bright idea struck him. He walked back to the fir-tree where he had rested, and found the lost missive. It had slipped out of his shirt when he shook himself. He was not particularly pleased. He knew that nobody would give him credit for his trouble in going back for it, or his astuteness in guessing where it was. He heaved the sigh of misunderstood genius, and again started for the post-office. This time he carried the letters openly and ostentatiously in his hand.

Presently he heard a voice say, "Hey!" It was a gentle, musical voice,—a stranger's voice, for it evidently did not know how to call him, and did not say, "Oh, Leonidas!" or "You—look here!" He was abreast of a little clearing, guarded by a low stockade of bark palings, and beyond it was a small white dwelling-house. Leonidas knew the place perfectly well. It belonged to the superintendent of a mining tunnel, who had lately rented it to some strangers from San Francisco. Thus much he had heard from his family. He had a mountain boy's contempt for city folks, and was not himself interested in them. Yet as he heard the call, he was conscious of a slightly guilty feeling. He might have been trespassing in following the rabbit's track; he might have been seen by some one when he lost the letter and had to go back for it—all grown-up people had a way of offering themselves as witnesses against him! He scowled a little as he glanced around him. Then his eye fell on the caller on the other side of the stockade.

To his surprise it was a woman: a pretty, gentle, fragile creature, all soft muslin and laces, with her fingers interlocked, and leaning both elbows on the top of the stockade as she stood under the checkered shadow of a buckeye.

"Come here—please—won't you?" she said pleasantly.

It would have been impossible to resist her voice if Leonidas had wanted to, which he didn't. He walked confidently up to the fence. She really was very pretty, with eyes like his setter's, and as caressing. And there were little puckers and satiny creases around her delicate nostrils and mouth when she spoke, which Leonidas knew were "expression."

"I—I"—she began, with charming hesitation; then suddenly, "What's your name?"

"Leonidas."

"Leonidas! That's a pretty name!" He thought it DID sound pretty. "Well, Leonidas, I want you to be a good boy and do a great favor for me,—a very great favor."

Leonidas's face fell. This kind of prelude and formula was familiar to him. It was usually followed by, "Promise me that you will never swear again," or, "that you will go straight home and wash your face," or some other irrelevant personality. But nobody with that sort of eyes had ever said it. So he said, a little shyly but sincerely, "Yes, ma'am."

"You are going to the post-office?"

This seemed a very foolish, womanish question, seeing that he was holding letters in his hand; but he said, "Yes."

"I want you to put a letter of mine among yours and post them all together," she said, putting one little hand to her bosom and drawing out a letter. He noticed that she purposely held the addressed side so that he could not see it, but he also noticed that her hand was small, thin, and white, even to a faint tint of blue in it, unlike his sister's, the baby's, or any other hand he had ever seen. "Can you read?" she said suddenly, withdrawing the letter.

The boy flushed slightly at the question. "Of course I can," he said proudly.

"Of course, certainly," she repeated quickly; "but," she added, with a mischievous smile, "you mustn't NOW! Promise me! Promise me that you won't read this address, but just post the letter, like one of your own, in the letter-box with the others."

Leonidas promised readily; it seemed to him a great fuss about nothing; perhaps it was some kind of game or a bet. He opened his sunburnt hand, holding his own letters, and she slipped hers, face downward, between them. Her soft fingers touched his in the operation, and seemed to leave a pleasant warmth behind them.

"Promise me another thing," she added; "promise me you won't say a word of this to any one."

"Of course!" said Leonidas.

"That's a good boy, and I know you will keep your word." She hesitated a moment, smilingly and tentatively, and then held out a bright half-dollar. Leonidas backed from the fence. "I'd rather not," he said shyly.

"But as a present from ME?"

Leonidas colored—he was really proud; and he was also bright enough to understand that the possession of such unbounded wealth would provoke dangerous inquiry at home. But he didn't like to say it, and only replied, "I can't."

She looked at him curiously. "Then—thank you," she said, offering her white hand, which felt like a bird in his. "Now run on, and don't let me keep you any longer." She drew back from the fence as she spoke, and waved him a pretty farewell. Leonidas, half sorry, half relieved, darted away.

He ran to the post-office, which he never had done before. Loyally he never looked at her letter, nor, indeed, at his own again, swinging the hand that held them far from his side. He entered the post-office directly, going at once to the letter-box and depositing the precious missive with the others. The post-office was also the "country store," and Leonidas was in the habit of still further protracting his errands there by lingering in that stimulating atmosphere of sugar, cheese, and coffee. But to-day his stay was brief, so transitory that the postmaster himself inferred audibly that "old man Boone must have been tanning Lee with a hickory switch." But the simple reason was that Leonidas wished to go back to the stockade fence and the fair stranger, if haply she was still there. His heart sank as, breathless with unwonted haste, he reached the clearing and the empty buckeye shade. He walked slowly and with sad diffidence by the deserted stockade fence. But presently his quick eye discerned a glint of white among the laurels near the house. It was SHE, walking with apparent indifference away from him towards the corner of the clearing and the road. But this he knew would bring her to the end of the stockade fence, where he must pass—and it did. She turned to him with a bright smile of affected surprise. "Why, you're as swift-footed as Mercury!"

Leonidas understood her perfectly. Mercury was the other name for quicksilver—and that was lively, you bet! He had often spilt some on the floor to see it move. She must be awfully cute to have noticed it too—cuter than his sisters. He was quite breathless with pleasure.

"I put your letter in the box all right," he burst out at last.

"Without any one seeing it?" she asked.

"Sure pop! nary one! The postmaster stuck out his hand to grab it, but I just let on that I didn't see him, and shoved it in myself."

"You're as sharp as you're good," she said smilingly. "Now, there's just ONE thing more I want you to do. Forget all about this—won't you?"

Her voice was very caressing. Perhaps that was why he said boldly: "Yes, ma'am, all except YOU."

"Dear me, what a compliment! How old are you?"

"Goin' on fifteen," said Leonidas confidently.

"And going very fast," said the lady mischievously. "Well, then, you needn't forget ME. On the contrary," she added, after looking at him curiously, "I would rather you'd remember me. Good-by—or, rather, good-afternoon—if I'm to be remembered, Leon."

"Good-afternoon, ma'am."

She moved away, and presently disappeared among the laurels. But her last words were ringing in his ears. "Leon"—everybody else called him "Lee" for brevity; "Leon"—it was pretty as she said it.

He turned away. But it so chanced that their parting was not to pass unnoticed, for, looking up the hill, Leonidas perceived his elder sister and little brother coming down the road, and knew that they must have seen him from the hilltop. It was like their "snoopin'"!

They ran to him eagerly.

"You were talking to the stranger," said his sister breathlessly.

"She spoke to me first," said Leonidas, on the defensive.

"What did she say?"

"Wanted to know the eleckshun news," said Leonidas with

cool mendacity, "and I told her."

This improbable fiction nevertheless satisfied them. "What was she like? Oh, do tell us, Lee!" continued his sister.

Nothing would have delighted him more than to expatiate upon her loveliness, the soft white beauty of her hands, the "cunning" little puckers around her lips, her bright tender eyes, the angelic texture of her robes, and the musical tinkle of her voice. But Leonidas had no confidant, and what healthy boy ever trusted his sister in such matter! "YOU saw what she was like," he said, with evasive bluntness.

"But, Lee"—

But Lee was adamant. "Go and ask her," he said.

"Like as not you were sassy to her, and she shut you up," said his sister artfully. But even this cruel suggestion, which he could have so easily flouted, did not draw him, and his ingenious relations flounced disgustedly away.

But Leonidas was not spared any further allusion to the fair stranger; for the fact of her having spoken to him was duly reported at home, and at dinner his reticence was again sorely attacked. "Just like her, in spite of all her airs and graces, to hang out along the fence like any ordinary hired girl, jabberin' with anybody that went along the road," said his mother incisively. He knew that she didn't like her new neighbors, so this did not surprise nor greatly pain him. Neither did the prosaic facts that were now first made plain to him. His divinity was a Mrs. Burroughs, whose husband was conducting a series of mining operations, and prospecting with a gang of men on the Casket Ridge. As his duty required his continual presence there, Mrs. Burroughs was forced to forego the civilized pleasures of San Francisco

Bret Harte

for a frontier life, for which she was ill fitted, and in which she had no interest. All this was a vague irrelevance to Leonidas, who knew her only as a goddess in white who had been familiar to him, and kind, and to whom he was tied by the delicious joy of having a secret in common, and having done her a special favor. Healthy youth clings to its own impressions, let reason, experience, and even facts argue ever to the contrary.

So he kept her secret and his intact, and was rewarded a few days afterwards by a distant view of her walking in the garden, with a man whom he recognized as her husband. It is needless to say that, without any extraneous thought, the man suffered in Leonidas's estimation by his propinquity to the goddess, and that he deemed him vastly inferior.

It was a still greater reward to his fidelity that she seized an opportunity when her husband's head was turned to wave her hand to him. Leonidas did not approach the fence, partly through shyness and partly through a more subtle instinct that this man was not in the secret. He was right, for only the next day, as he passed to the post-office, she called him to the fence.

"Did you see me wave my hand to you yesterday?" she asked pleasantly.

"Yes, ma'am; but"—he hesitated—"I didn't come up, for I didn't think you wanted me when any one else was there."

She laughed merrily, and lifting his straw hat from his head, ran the fingers of the other hand through his damp curls. "You're the brightest, dearest boy I ever knew, Leon," she said, dropping her pretty face to the level of his own, "and I ought to have remembered it. But I don't mind telling you I was dreadfully frightened lest you might misunderstand me and come and ask for another letter—before HIM." As she emphasized the personal pronoun, her whole face seemed to change: the light of her blue eyes became mere glittering points, her nostrils grew white and contracted, and her pretty little mouth seemed to narrow into a straight cruel line, like a cat's. "Not a word ever to HIM, of all men! Do you hear?" she said almost brusquely. Then, seeing the concern in the boy's face, she laughed, and added explanatorily: "He's a bad, bad man, Leon, remember that."

The fact that she was speaking of her husband did not shock the boy's moral sense in the least. The sacredness of those relations, and even of blood kinship, is, I fear, not always so clear to the youthful mind as we fondly imagine. That Mr. Burroughs was a bad man to have excited this change in this lovely woman was Leonidas's only conclusion. He remembered how his sister's soft, pretty little kitten, purring on her lap, used to get its back up and spit at the postmaster's yellow hound.

"I never wished to come unless you called me first," he said frankly.

"What?" she said, in her half playful, half reproachful, but wholly caressing way. "You mean to say you would never come to see me unless I sent for you? Oh, Leon! and you'd abandon me in that way?"

But Leonidas was set in his own boyish superstition. "I'd just delight in being sent for by you any time, Mrs. Burroughs, and you kin always find me," he said shyly, but doggedly; "but"—He stopped.

"What an opinionated young gentleman! Well, I see I must do all the courting. So consider that I sent for you this morning. I've got another letter for you to mail." She put her hand to her breast, and out of the pretty frillings of her frock produced, as before, with the same faint perfume of violets, a letter like the first. But it was unsealed. "Now, listen, Leon; we are going to be great friends—you and I." Leonidas felt his cheeks glowing. "You are going to do me another great favor, and we are going to have a little fun and a great secret all by our own selves. Now, first, have you any correspondent—you know—any one who writes to you—any boy or girl—from San Francisco?"

Leonidas's cheeks grew redder—alas! from a less happy consciousness. He never received any letters; nobody ever wrote to him. He was obliged to make this shameful admission.

Mrs. Burroughs looked thoughtful. "But you have some friend in San Francisco—some one who MIGHT write to you?" she suggested pleasantly.

"I knew a boy once who went to San Francisco," said Leonidas doubtfully. "At least, he allowed he was goin' there."

"That will do," said Mrs. Burroughs. "I suppose your parents know him or of him?"

"Why," said Leonidas, "he used to live here."

"Better still. For, you see, it wouldn't be strange if he DID write. What was the gentleman's name?"

"Jim Belcher," returned Leonidas hesitatingly, by no means sure that the absent Belcher knew how to write. Mrs. Burroughs took a tiny pencil from her belt, opened the letter she was holding in her hand, and apparently wrote the name in it. Then she folded it and sealed it, smiling charmingly at

Leonidas's puzzled face.

"Now, Leon, listen; for here is the favor I am asking. Mr. Jim Belcher"—she pronounced the name with great gravity—"will write to you in a few days. But inside of YOUR letter will be a little note to me, which you will bring me. You can show your letter to your family, if they want to know who it is from; but no one must see MINE. Can you manage that?"

"Yes," said Leonidas. Then, as the whole idea flashed upon his quick intelligence, he smiled until he showed his dimples. Mrs. Burroughs leaned forward over the fence, lifted his torn straw hat, and dropped a fluttering little kiss on his forehead. It seemed to the boy, flushed and rosy as a maid, as if she had left a shining star there for every one to see.

"Don't smile like that, Leon, you're positively irresistible! It will be a nice little game, won't it? Nobody in it but you and me—and Belcher! We'll outwit them yet. And, you see, you'll be obliged to come to me, after all, without my asking."

They both laughed; indeed, quite a dimpled, bright-eyed, rosy, innocent pair, though I think Leonidas was the more maidenly.

"And," added Leonidas, with breathless eagerness, "I can sometimes write to—to—Jim, and inclose your letter."

"Angel of wisdom! certainly. Well, now, let's see—have you got any letters for the post to-day?" He colored again, for in anticipation of meeting her he had hurried up the family post that morning. He held out his letters: she thrust her own among them. "Now," she said, laying her cool, soft hand against his hot cheek, "run along, dear; you must not be seen loitering here."

Leonidas ran off, buoyed up on ambient air. It seemed just like a fairy-book. Here he was, the confidant of the most beautiful creature he had seen, and there was a mysterious letter coming to him—Leonidas—and no one to know why. And now he had a "call" to see her often; she would not forget him—he needn't loiter by the fencepost to see if she wanted him—and his boyish pride and shyness were appeased. There was no question of moral ethics raised in Leonidas's mind; he knew that it would not be the real Jim Belcher who would write to him, but that made the prospect the more attractive. Nor did another circumstance trouble his conscience. When he reached the post-office, he was surprised to see the man whom he knew to be Mr. Burroughs talking with the postmaster. Leonidas brushed by him and deposited his letters in the box in discreet triumph. The postmaster was evidently officially resenting some imputation on his carelessness, and, concluding his defense, "No, sir," he said, "you kin bet your boots that ef any letter hez gone astray for you or your wife— Ye said your wife, didn't ye?"

"Yes," said Burroughs hastily, with a glance around the shop.

"Well, for you or anybody at your house—it ain't here that's the fault. You hear me! I know every letter that comes in and goes outer this office, I reckon, and handle 'em all,"— Leonidas pricked up his ears,—"and if anybody oughter know, it's me. Ye kin paste that in your hat, Mr. Burroughs." Burroughs, apparently disconcerted by the intrusion of a third party—Leonidas—upon what was evidently a private inquiry, murmured something surlily, and passed out.

Leonidas was puzzled. That big man seemed to be "snoopin'" around for something! He knew that he dared not touch the letter-bag,—Leonidas had heard somewhere that it was a deadly crime to touch any letters after the Government had got hold of them once, and he had no fears for the safety of hers. But ought he not go back at once and tell her about her husband's visit, and the alarming fact that the postmaster was personally acquainted with all the letters? He instantly saw, too, the wisdom of her inclosing her letter hereafter in another address. Yet he finally resolved not to tell her to-day,—it would look like "hanging round" again; and—another secret reason—he was afraid that any allusion to her husband's interference would bring back that change in her beautiful face which he did not like. The better to resist temptation, he went back another way.

It must not be supposed that, while Leonidas indulged in this secret passion for the beautiful stranger, it was to the exclusion of his boyish habits. It merely took the place of his intellectual visions and his romantic reading. He no longer carried books in his pocket on his lazy rambles. What were mediaeval legends of high-born ladies and their pages to this real romance of himself and Mrs. Burroughs? What were the exploits of boy captains and juvenile trappers and the Indian maidens and Spanish senoritas to what was now possible to himself and his divinity here—upon Casket Ridge! The very ground around her was now consecrated to romance and adventure. Consequently, he visited a few traps on his way back which he had set for "jackass-rabbits" and wildcats,—the latter a vindictive reprisal for aggression upon an orphan brood of mountain quail which he had taken under his protection. For, while he nourished a keen love of sport, it was controlled by a boy's larger understanding of nature: a pantheistic sympathy with man and beast and plant, which made him keenly alive to the strange cruelties of creation, revealed to him some queer animal feuds, and made him a chivalrous partisan of the weaker. He had even gone out of his way to defend, by ingenious contrivances of his own, the hoard of a golden squirrel and the treasures of some wild bees from a predatory bear, although it did not prevent him later from capturing the squirrel by an equally ingenious contrivance, and from eventually eating some of the honey.

He was late home that evening. But this was "vacation,"—the district school was closed, and but for the household "chores," which occupied his early mornings, each long summer day was a holiday. So two or three passed; and then one morning, on his going to the post-office, the postmaster threw down upon the counter a real and rather bulky letter, duly stamped, and addressed to Mr. Leonidas Boone! Leonidas was too discreet to open it before witnesses, but in the solitude of the trail home broke the seal. It contained another letter with no address—clearly the one SHE expected—and, more marvelous still, a sheaf of trout-hooks, with delicate gut-snells such as Leonidas had only dared to dream of. The letter to himself was written in a clear, distinct hand, and ran as follows:—

DEAR LEE,—How are you getting on on old Casket Ridge? It seems a coon's age since you and me was together, and times I get to think I must just run up and see you! We're having bully times in 'Frisco, you bet! though there ain't anything wild worth shucks to go to see—'cept the sea lions at the Cliff House. They're just stunning—big as a grizzly, and bigger—climbing over a big rock or swimming in the sea like an otter or muskrat. I'm sending you some snells and hooks, such as you can't get at Casket. Use the fine ones for pot-holes and the bigger ones for running water or falls. Let me know when you've got 'em. Write to Lock Box No. 1290. That's where dad's letters come. So no more at present.

From yours truly,

JIM BELCHER.

Not only did Leonidas know that this was not from the real Jim, but he felt the vague contact of a new, charming, and original personality that fascinated him. Of course, it was only natural that one of HER friends—as he must be—should be equally delightful. There was no jealousy in Leonidas's devotion; he knew only a joy in this fellowship of admiration for her which he was satisfied that the other boy must feel. And only the right kind of boy could know the importance of his ravishing gift, and this Jim was evidently "no slouch"! Yet, in Leonidas's new joy he did not forget HER! He ran back to the stockade fence and lounged upon the road in view of the house, but she did not appear.

Leonidas lingered on the top of the hill, ostentatiously examining a young hickory for a green switch, but to no effect. Then it suddenly occurred to him that she might be staying in purposely, and, perhaps a little piqued by her indifference, he ran off. There was a mountain stream hard by, now dwindled in the summer drouth to a mere trickling thread among the boulders, and there was a certain "pot-hole" that he had long known. It was the lurking-place of a phenomenal trout,—an almost historic fish in the district, which had long resisted the attempt of such rude sportsmen as miners, or even experts like himself. Few had seen it, except as a vague, shadowy bulk in the four feet of depth and gloom in which it hid; only once had Leonidas's quick eye feasted on its fair proportions. On that memorable occasion Leonidas, having exhausted every kind of lure of painted fly and living bait, was rising from his knees behind the bank, when a pink five-cent stamp dislodged from his pocket fluttered in the air, and descended slowly upon the still pool. Horrified at his loss, Leonidas leaned over to recover it, when there was a flash like lightning in the black depths, a dozen changes of light and shadow on the surface, a little whirling wave splashing against the side of the rock, and the postage stamp was gone. More than that—for one instant the trout remained visible, stationary and expectant! Whether it was the instinct of sport, or whether the fish had detected a

Bret Harte

new, subtle, and original flavor in the gum and paper, Leonidas never knew. Alas! he had not another stamp; he was obliged to leave the fish, but carried a brilliant idea away with him. Ever since then he had cherished it—and another extra stamp in his pocket. And now, with this strong but gossamer-like snell, this new hook, and this freshly cut hickory rod, he would make the trial!

But fate was against him! He had scarcely descended the narrow trail to the pine-fringed margin of the stream before his quick ear detected an unusual rustling through the adjacent underbrush, and then a voice that startled him! It was HERS! In an instant all thought of sport had fled. With a beating heart, half opened lips, and uplifted lashes, Leonidas awaited the coming of his divinity like a timorous virgin at her first tryst.

But Mrs. Burroughs was clearly not in an equally responsive mood. With her fair face reddened by the sun, the damp tendrils of her unwound hair clinging to her forehead, and her smart little slippers red with dust, there was also a querulous light in her eyes, and a still more querulous pinch in her nostrils, as she stood panting before him.

"You tiresome boy!" she gasped, holding one little hand to her side as she gripped her brambled skirt around her ankles with the other. "Why didn't you wait? Why did you make me run all this distance after you?"

Leonidas timidly and poignantly protested. He had waited before the house and on the hill; he thought she didn't want him.

"Couldn't you see that THAT MAN kept me in?" she went on peevishly. "Haven't you sense enough to know that he suspects something, and follows me everywhere, dogging my footsteps every time the post comes in, and even going to the post-office himself, to make sure that he sees all my letters? Well," she added impatiently, "have you anything for me? Why don't you speak?"

Crushed and remorseful, Leonidas produced her letter. She almost snatched it from his hand, opened it, read a few lines, and her face changed. A smile strayed from her eyes to her lips, and back again. Leonidas's heart was lifted; she was so forgiving and so beautiful!

"Is he a boy, Mrs. Burroughs?" asked Leonidas shyly.

"Well—not exactly," she said, her charming face all radiant again. "He's older than you. What has he written to you?"

Leonidas put his letter in her hand for reply.

"I wish I could see him, you know," he said shyly. "That letter's bully—it's just rats! I like him pow'ful."

Mrs. Burroughs had skimmed through the letter, but not interestedly.

"You mustn't like him more than you like me," she said laughingly, caressing him with her voice and eyes, and even her straying hand.

"I couldn't do that! I never could like anybody as I like you," said. Leonidas gravely. There was such appalling truthfulness in the boy's voice and frankly opened eyes that the woman could not evade it, and was slightly disconcerted. But she presently started up with a vexatious cry. "There's that wretch following me again, I do believe," she said, staring at the hilltop. "Yes! Look, Leon, he's turning to come down this trail. What's to be done? He mustn't see me here!"

Leonidas looked. It was indeed Mr. Burroughs; but he was evidently only taking a short cut towards the Ridge, where his men were working. Leonidas had seen him take it before. But it was the principal trail on the steep hillside, and they must eventually meet. A man might evade it by scrambling through the brush to a lower and rougher trail; but a woman, never! But an idea had seized Leonidas. "I can stop him," he said confidently to her. "You just lie low here behind that rock till I come back. He hasn't seen you yet."

She had barely time to draw back before Leonidas darted down the trail towards her husband. Yet, in her intense curiosity, she leaned out the next moment to watch him. He paused at last, not far from the approaching figure, and seemed to kneel down on the trail. What was he doing? Her husband was still slowly advancing. Suddenly he stopped. At the same moment she heard their two voices in excited parley, and then, to her amazement, she saw her husband scramble hurriedly down the trail to the lower level, and with an occasional backward glance, hasten away until he had passed beyond her view.

She could scarcely realize her narrow escape when Leonidas stood by her side. "How did you do it?" she said eagerly.

"With a rattler!" said the boy gravely.

"With a what?"

"A rattlesnake—pizen snake, you know."

"A rattlesnake?" she said, staring at Leonidas with a quick snatching away of her skirts.

The boy, who seemed to have forgotten her in his other abstraction of adventure, now turned quickly, with devoted eyes and a reassuring smile.

"Yes; but I wouldn't let him hurt you," he said gently.

"But what did you DO?"

He looked at her curiously. "You won't be frightened if I show you?" he said doubtfully. "There's nothin' to be afeerd of s'long as you're with me," he added proudly.

"Yes—that is"—she stammered, and then, her curiosity getting the better of her fear, she added in a whisper: "Show me quick!"

He led the way up the narrow trail until he stopped where he had knelt before. It was a narrow, sunny ledge of rock, scarcely wide enough for a single person to pass. He silently pointed to a cleft in the rock, and kneeling down again, began to whistle in a soft, fluttering way. There was a moment of suspense, and then she was conscious of an awful gliding something,—a movement so measured yet so exquisitely graceful that she stood enthralled. A narrow, flattened, expressionless head was followed by a footlong strip of yellow-barred scales; then there was a pause, and the head turned, in a beautifully symmetrical half-circle, towards the whistler. The whistling ceased; the snake, with half its body out of the cleft, remained poised in air as if stiffened to stone.

"There," said Leonidas quietly, "that's what Mr. Burroughs saw, and that's WHY he scooted off the trail. I just called out William Henry,—I call him William Henry, and he knows his name,—and then I sang out to Mr. Burroughs what was up; and it was lucky I did, for the next moment he'd have been on top of him and have been struck, for rattlers don't give way to any one."

Bret Harte

"Oh, why didn't you let"—She stopped herself quickly, but could not stop the fierce glint in her eye nor the sharp curve in her nostril. Luckily, Leonidas did not see this, being preoccupied with his other graceful charmer, William Henry.

"But how did you know it was here?" said Mrs. Burroughs, recovering herself.

"Fetched him here," said Leonidas briefly.

"What in your hands?" she said, drawing back.

"No! made him follow! I HAVE handled him, but it was after I'd first made him strike his pizen out upon a stick. Ye know, after he strikes four times he ain't got any pizen left. Then ye kin do anythin' with him, and he knows it. He knows me, you bet! I've bin three months trainin' him. Look! Don't be frightened," he said, as Mrs. Burroughs drew hurriedly back; "see him mind me. Now scoot home, William Henry."

He accompanied the command with a slow, dominant movement of the hickory rod he was carrying. The snake dropped its head, and slid noiselessly out of the cleft across the trail and down the hill.

"Thinks my rod is witch-hazel, which rattlers can't abide," continued Leonidas, dropping into a boy's breathless abbreviated speech. "Lives down your way—just back of your farm. Show ye some day. Suns himself on a flat stone every day—always cold—never can get warm. Eh?"

She had not spoken, but was gazing into space with a breathless rigidity of attitude and a fixed look in her eye, not unlike the motionless orbs of the reptile that had glided away.

"Does anybody else know you keep him?" she asked.

"Nary one. I never showed him to anybody but you," replied the boy.

"Don't! You must show me where he hides to-morrow," she said, in her old laughing way. "And now, Leon, I must go back to the house."

"May I write to him—to Jim Belcher, Mrs. Burroughs?" said the boy timidly.

"Certainly. And come to me to-morrow with your letter—I will have mine ready. Good-by." She stopped and glanced at the trail. "And you say that if that man had kept on, the snake would have bitten him?"

"Sure pop!—if he'd trod on him—as he was sure to. The snake wouldn't have known he didn't mean it. It's only natural," continued Leonidas, with glowing partisanship for the gentle and absent William Henry. "YOU wouldn't like to be trodden upon, Mrs. Burroughs!"

"No! I'd strike out!" she said quickly. She made a rapid motion forward with her low forehead and level head, leaving it rigid the next moment, so that it reminded him of the snake, and he laughed. At which she laughed too, and tripped away.

Leonidas went back and caught his trout. But even this triumph did not remove a vague sense of disappointment which had come over him. He had often pictured to himself a Heaven-sent meeting with her in the woods, a walk with her, alone, where he could pick her the rarest flowers and herbs and show her his woodland friends; and it had only ended in this, and an exhibition of William Henry! He ought to have saved HER from something, and not her husband. Yet he had no ill-feeling for Burroughs, only a desire to circumvent him, on behalf of the unprotected, as he would have baffled a hawk or a wildcat. He went home in dismal spirits, but later that evening constructed a boyish letter of thanks to the apocryphal Belcher and told him all about—the trout!

He brought her his letter the next day, and received hers to inclose. She was pleasant, her own charming self again, but she seemed more interested in other things than himself, as, for instance, the docile William Henry, whose hiding-place he showed, and whose few tricks she made him exhibit to her, and which the gratified Leonidas accepted as a delicate form of flattery to himself. But his yearning, innocent spirit detected a something lacking, which he was too proud to admit even to himself. It was his own fault; he ought to have waited for her, and not gone for the trout!

So a fortnight passed with an interchange of the vicarious letters, and brief, hopeful, and disappointing meetings to Leonidas. To add to his unhappiness, he was obliged to listen to sneering disparagement of his goddess from his family, and criticisms which, happily, his innocence did not comprehend. It was his own mother who accused her of shamefully "making up" to the good-looking expressman at church last Sunday, and declared that Burroughs ought to "look after that wife of his,"—two statements which the simple Leonidas could not reconcile. He had seen the incident, and only thought her more lovely than ever. Why should not the expressman think so too? And yet the boy was not happy; something intruded upon his sports, upon his books, making them dull and vapid, and yet that something was she! He grew pale and preoccupied. If he had only some one in whom to confide—some one who could explain his hopes and fears. That one was nearer than he thought!

It was quite three weeks since the rattlesnake incident, and he was wandering moodily over Casket Ridge. He was near the Casket, that abrupt upheaval of quartz and gneiss, shaped like a coffer, from which the mountain took its name. It was a favorite haunt of Leonidas, one of whose boyish superstitions was that it contained a treasure of gold, and one of whose brightest dreams had been that he should yet discover it. This he did not do to-day, but looking up from the rocks that he was listlessly examining, he made the almost as thrilling discovery that near him on the trail was a distinguished-looking stranger.

He was bestriding a shapely mustang, which well became his handsome face and slight, elegant figure, and he was looking at Leonidas with an amused curiosity and a certain easy assurance that were difficult to withstand. It was with the same fascinating self-confidence of smile, voice, and manner that he rode up to the boy, and leaning lightly over his saddle, said with exaggerated politeness: "I believe I have the pleasure of addressing Mr. Leonidas Boone?"

The rising color in Leonidas's face was apparently a sufficient answer to the stranger, for he continued smilingly, "Then permit me to introduce myself as Mr. James Belcher. As you perceive, I have grown considerably since you last saw me. In fact, I've done nothing else. It's surprising what a fellow can do when he sets his mind on one thing. And then, you know, they're always telling you that San Francisco is a 'growing place.' That accounts for it!"

Leonidas, dazed, dazzled, but delighted, showed all his white teeth in a shy laugh. At which the enchanting stranger leaped from his horse like a very boy, drew his arm through the rein, and going up to Leonidas, lifted the boy's straw hat from his head and ran his fingers through his curls. There was nothing original in that—everybody did that to him as a preliminary to conversation. But when this ingenuous fine gentleman put his own Panama hat on Leonidas's head, and clapped Leonidas's torn straw on his own, and, passing his arm through the boy's, began to walk on with him, Leonidas's simple heart went out to him at once.

"And now, Leon," said the delightful stranger, "let's you and me have a talk. There's a nice cool spot under these laurels; I'll stake out Pepita, and we'll just lie off there and gab, and not care if school keeps or not."

"But you know you ain't really Jim Belcher," said the boy shyly.

"I'm as good a man as he is any day, whoever I am," said the stranger, with humorous defiance, "and can lick him out of his boots, whoever HE is. That ought to satisfy you. But if you want my certificate, here's your own letter, old man," he said, producing Leonidas's last scrawl from his pocket.

"And HERS?" said the boy cautiously.

The stranger's face changed a little. "And HERS," he repeated gravely, showing a little pink note which Leonidas recognized as one of Mrs. Burroughs's inclosures. The boy was silent until they reached the laurels, where the stranger tethered his horse and then threw himself in an easy attitude beneath the tree, with the back of his head upon his clasped hands. Leonidas could see his curved brown mustaches and silky lashes that were almost as long, and thought him the handsomest man he had ever beheld.

"Well, Leon," said the stranger, stretching himself out comfortably and pulling the boy down beside him, "how are things going on the Casket? All serene, eh?"

The inquiry so dismally recalled Leonidas's late feelings that his face clouded, and he involuntarily sighed. The stranger instantly shifted his head and gazed curiously at him. Then he took the boy's sunburnt hand in his own, and held it a moment. "Well, go on," he said.

"Well, Mr.—Mr.—I can't go on—I won't!" said Leonidas, with a sudden fit of obstinacy. "I don't know what to call you."

"Call me 'Jack'—'Jack Hamlin' when you're not in a hurry. Ever heard of me before?" he added, suddenly turning his head towards Leonidas.

The boy shook his head. "No."

Mr. Jack Hamlin lifted his lashes in affected expostulation to the skies. "And this is Fame!" he murmured audibly.

But this Leonidas did not comprehend. Nor could he understand why the stranger, who clearly must have come to see HER, should not ask about her, should not rush to seek her, but should lie back there all the while so contentedly on the grass. HE wouldn't. He half resented it, and then it occurred to him that this fine gentleman was like himself—shy. Who could help being so before such an angel? HE would help him on.

And so, shyly at first, but bit by bit emboldened by a word or two from Jack, he began to talk of her—of her beauty—of her kindness—of his own unworthiness—of what she had said and done—until, finding in this gracious stranger the vent his pent-up feelings so long had sought, he sang then and there the little idyl of his boyish life. He told of his decline in her affections after his unpardonable sin in keeping her waiting while he went for the trout, and added the miserable mistake of the rattlesnake episode. "For it was a mistake, Mr. Hamlin. I oughtn't to have let a lady like that know anything about snakes—just because I happen to know them."

"It WAS an awful slump, Lee," said Hamlin gravely. "Get a woman and a snake together—and where are you? Think of Adam and Eve and the serpent, you know."

"But it wasn't that way," said the boy earnestly. "And I want to tell you something else that's just makin' me sick, Mr. Hamlin. You know I told you William Henry lives down at the bottom of Burroughs's garden, and how I showed Mrs. Burroughs his tricks! Well, only two days ago I was down there looking for him, and couldn't find him anywhere. There's a sort of narrow trail from the garden to the hill, a short cut up to the Ridge, instead o' going by their gate. It's just the trail any one would take in a hurry, or if they didn't want to be seen from the road. Well! I was looking this way and that for William Henry, and whistlin' for him, when I slipped on to the trail. There, in the middle of it, was an old bucket turned upside down—just the thing a man would kick away or a woman lift up. Well, Mr. Hamlin, I kicked it away, and"—the boy stopped, with rounded eyes and bated breath, and added—"I just had time to give one jump and save myself! For under that pail, cramped down so he couldn't get out, and just bilin' over with rage, and chockful of pizen, was William Henry! If it had been anybody else less spry, they'd have got bitten,—and that's just what the sneak who put it there knew."

Mr. Hamlin uttered an exclamation under his breath, and rose to his feet.

"What did you say?" asked the boy quickly.

"Nothing," said Mr. Hamlin.

But it had sounded to Leonidas like an oath.

Mr. Hamlin walked a few steps, as if stretching his limbs, and then said: "And you think Burroughs would have been bitten?"

"Why, no!" said Leonidas in astonished indignation; "of course not—not BURROUGHS. It would have been poor MRS. Burroughs. For, of course, HE set that trap for her— don't you see? Who else would do it?"

"Of course, of course! Certainly," said Mr. Hamlin coolly. "Of course, as you say, HE set the trap—yes—you just hang on to that idea."

But something in Mr. Hamlin's manner, and a peculiar look in his eye, did not satisfy Leonidas. "Are you going to see her now?" he said eagerly. "I can show you the house, and then run in and tell her you're outside in the laurels."

"Not just yet," said Mr. Hamlin, laying his hand on the boy's head after having restored his own hat. "You see, I thought of giving her a surprise. A big surprise!" he added slowly. After a pause, he went on: "Did you tell her what you had seen?"

"Of course I did," said Leonidas reproachfully. "Did you think I was going to let her get bit? It might have killed her."

"And it might not have been an unmixed pleasure for William Henry. I mean," said Mr. Hamlin gravely, correcting himself, "YOU would never have forgiven him. But what did she say?"

The boy's face clouded. "She thanked me and said it was very thoughtful—and kind—though it might have been only an accident"—he stammered—"and then she said perhaps I was hanging round and coming there a little too much lately, and that as Burroughs was very watchful, I'd better quit for two or three days." The tears were rising to his eyes, but by putting his two clenched fists into his pockets, he managed to hold them down. Perhaps Mr. Hamlin's soft hand on his head assisted him. Mr. Hamlin took from his pocket a notebook, and tearing out a leaf, sat down again and began to write on his knee. After a pause, Leonidas said,—

"Was you ever in love, Mr. Hamlin?"

"Never," said Mr. Hamlin, quietly continuing to write. "But, now you speak of it, it's a long-felt want in my nature that I intend to supply some day. But not until I've made my pile. And don't YOU either." He continued writing, for it was this gentleman's peculiarity to talk without apparently the slightest concern whether anybody else spoke, whether he was listened to, or whether his remarks were at all relevant to the case. Yet he was always listened to for that reason. When he had finished writing, he folded up the paper, put it in an envelope, and addressed it.

"Shall I take it to her?" said Leonidas eagerly.

"It's not for HER; it's for him—Mr. Burroughs," said Mr. Hamlin quietly.

The boy drew back. "To get him out of the way," added Hamlin explanatorily. "When he gets it, lightning wouldn't keep him here. Now, how to send it," he said thoughtfully.

"You might leave it at the post-office," said Leonidas timidly. "He always goes there to watch his wife's letters."

For the first time in their interview Mr. Hamlin distinctly laughed.

"Your head is level, Leo, and I'll do it. Now the best thing you can do is to follow Mrs. Burroughs's advice. Quit going to the house for a day or two." He walked towards his horse. The boy's face sank, but he kept up bravely. "And will I see you again?" he said wistfully.

Mr. Hamlin lowered his face so near the boy's that Leonidas could see himself in the brown depths of Mr. Hamlin's eyes. "I hope you will," he said gravely. He mounted, shook the boy's hand, and rode away in the lengthening shadows. Then Leonidas walked sadly home.

There was no need for him to keep his promise; for the next morning the family were stirred by the announcement that Mr. and Mrs. Burroughs had left Casket Ridge that night by the down stage for Sacramento, and that the house was closed. There were various rumors concerning the reason of this sudden departure, but only one was persistent, and borne out by the postmaster. It was that Mr. Burroughs had received that afternoon an anonymous note that his wife was about to elope with the notorious San Francisco gambler, Jack Hamlin.

But Leonidas Boone, albeit half understanding, kept his miserable secret with a still hopeful and trustful heart. It grieved him a little that William Henry was found a few days later dead, with his head crushed. Yet it was not until years later, when he had made a successful "prospect" on Casket Ridge, that he met Mr. Hamlin in San Francisco, and knew how he had played the part of Mercury upon that "heaven-kissing hill."

COLONEL STARBOTTLE FOR THE PLAINTIFF

It had been a day of triumph for Colonel Starbottle. First, for his personality, as it would have been difficult to separate the Colonel's achievements from his individuality; second, for his oratorical abilities as a sympathetic pleader; and third, for his functions as the leading legal counsel for the Eureka Ditch Company versus the State of California. On his strictly legal performances in this issue I prefer not to speak; there were those who denied them, although the jury had accepted them in the face of the ruling of the half amused, half cynical Judge himself. For an hour they had laughed with the Colonel, wept with him, been stirred to personal indignation or patriotic exaltation by his passionate and lofty periods,— what else could they do than give him their verdict? If it was alleged by some that the American eagle, Thomas Jefferson, and the Resolutions of '98 had nothing whatever to do with the contest of a ditch company over a doubtfully worded legislative document; that wholesale abuse of the State Attorney and his political motives had not the slightest connection with the legal question raised—it was, neverthe- less, generally accepted that the losing party would have been only too glad to have the Colonel on their side. And Colonel Starbottle knew this, as, perspiring, florid, and panting, he rebuttoned the lower buttons of his blue frock- coat, which had become loosed in an oratorical spasm, and readjusted his old-fashioned, spotless shirt frill above it as he strutted from the court-room amidst the handshakings and acclamations of his friends.

And here an unprecedented thing occurred. The Colonel absolutely declined spirituous refreshment at the neighboring Palmetto Saloon, and declared his intention of proceeding directly to his office in the adjoining square. Nevertheless, the Colonel quitted the building alone, and apparently unarmed, except for his faithful gold-headed stick, which hung as usual from his forearm. The crowd gazed after him with undisguised admiration of this new evidence of his pluck. It was remembered also that a mysterious note had been handed to him at the conclusion of his speech,— evidently a challenge from the State Attorney. It was quite plain that the Colonel—a practiced duelist—was hastening home to answer it.

But herein they were wrong. The note was in a female hand, and simply requested the Colonel to accord an interview with the writer at the Colonel's office as soon as he left the court. But it was an engagement that the Colonel—as devoted to the fair sex as he was to the "code"—was no less prompt in accepting. He flicked away the dust from his spotless white trousers and varnished boots with his handkerchief, and settled his black cravat under his Byron collar as he neared his office. He was surprised, however, on opening the door of his private office, to find his visitor already there; he was still more startled to find her somewhat past middle age and plainly attired. But the Colonel was brought up in a school of Southern politeness, already antique in the republic, and his bow of courtesy belonged to the epoch of his shirt frill and strapped trousers. No one could have detected his disappointment in his manner, albeit his sentences were short and incomplete. But the Colonel's colloquial speech was apt to be fragmentary incoherencies of his larger oratorical utterances.

"A thousand pardons—for—er—having kept a lady waiting—
er! But—er—congratulations of friends—and—er—courtesy
due to them—er—interfered with—though perhaps only
heightened—by procrastination—the pleasure of—ha!" And
the Colonel completed his sentence with a gallant wave of his
fat but white and well-kept hand.

"Yes! I came to see you along o' that speech of yours. I was
in court. When I heard you gettin' it off on that jury, I says to
myself, 'That's the kind o' lawyer I want. A man that's
flowery and convincin'! Just the man to take up our case."

"Ah! It's a matter of business, I see," said the Colonel,
inwardly relieved, but externally careless. "And—er—may I
ask the nature of the case?"

"Well! it's a breach-o'-promise suit," said the visitor calmly.

If the Colonel had been surprised before, he was now really
startled, and with an added horror that required all his
politeness to conceal. Breach-of-promise cases were his
peculiar aversion. He had always held them to be a kind of
litigation which could have been obviated by the prompt
killing of the masculine offender—in which case he would
have gladly defended the killer. But a suit for damages,—
DAMAGES!—with the reading of love-letters before a
hilarious jury and court, was against all his instincts. His
chivalry was outraged; his sense of humor was small, and in
the course of his career he had lost one or two important cases
through an unexpected development of this quality in a jury.

The woman had evidently noticed his hesitation, but mistook
its cause. "It ain't me—but my darter."

The Colonel recovered his politeness. "Ah! I am relieved, my
dear madam! I could hardly conceive a man ignorant enough

to—er—er—throw away such evident good fortune—or base enough to deceive the trustfulness of womanhood—matured and experienced only in the chivalry of our sex, ha!"

The woman smiled grimly. "Yes!—it's my darter, Zaidee Hooker—so ye might spare some of them pretty speeches for HER—before the jury."

The Colonel winced slightly before this doubtful prospect, but smiled. "Ha! Yes!—certainly—the jury. But—er—my dear lady, need we go as far as that? Can not this affair be settled—er—out of court? Could not this—er—individual—be admonished—told that he must give satisfaction—personal satisfaction—for his dastardly conduct—to—er—near relative—or even valued personal friend? The—er—arrangements necessary for that purpose I myself would undertake."

He was quite sincere; indeed, his small black eyes shone with that fire which a pretty woman or an "affair of honor" could alone kindle. The visitor stared vacantly at him, and said slowly, "And what good is that goin' to do US?"

"Compel him to—er—perform his promise," said the Colonel, leaning back in his chair.

"Ketch him doin' it!" she exclaimed scornfully. "No—that ain't wot we're after. We must make him PAY! Damages—and nothin' short o' THAT."

The Colonel bit his lip. "I suppose," he said gloomily, "you have documentary evidence—written promises and protestations—er—er love-letters, in fact?"

"No—nary a letter! Ye see, that's jest it—and that's where YOU come in. You've got to convince that jury yourself.

You've got to show what it is—tell the whole story your own way. Lord! to a man like you that's nothin'."

Startling as this admission might have been to any other lawyer, Starbottle was absolutely relieved by it. The absence of any mirth-provoking correspondence, and the appeal solely to his own powers of persuasion, actually struck his fancy. He lightly put aside the compliment with a wave of his white hand.

"Of course," he said confidently, "there is strongly presumptive and corroborative evidence? Perhaps you can give me—er—a brief outline of the affair?"

"Zaidee kin do that straight enough, I reckon," said the woman; "what I want to know first is, kin you take the case?"

The Colonel did not hesitate; his curiosity was piqued. "I certainly can. I have no doubt your daughter will put me in possession of sufficient facts and details—to constitute what we call—er—a brief."

"She kin be brief enough—or long enough—for the matter of that," said the woman, rising. The Colonel accepted this implied witticism with a smile.

"And when may I have the pleasure of seeing her?" he asked politely.

"Well, I reckon as soon as I can trot out and call her. She's just outside, meanderin' in the road—kinder shy, ye know, at first."

She walked to the door. The astounded Colonel nevertheless gallantly accompanied her as she stepped out into the street and called shrilly, "You Zaidee!"

A young girl here apparently detached herself from a tree and the ostentatious perusal of an old election poster, and sauntered down towards the office door. Like her mother, she was plainly dressed; unlike her, she had a pale, rather refined face, with a demure mouth and downcast eyes. This was all the Colonel saw as he bowed profoundly and led the way into his office, for she accepted his salutations without lifting her head. He helped her gallantly to a chair, on which she seated herself sideways, somewhat ceremoniously, with her eyes following the point of her parasol as she traced a pattern on the carpet. A second chair offered to the mother that lady, however, declined. "I reckon to leave you and Zaidee together to talk it out," she said; turning to her daughter, she added, "Jest you tell him all, Zaidee," and before the Colonel could rise again, disappeared from the room. In spite of his professional experience, Starbottle was for a moment embarrassed. The young girl, however, broke the silence without looking up.

"Adoniram K. Hotchkiss," she began, in a monotonous voice, as if it were a recitation addressed to the public, "first began to take notice of me a year ago. Arter that—off and on"—

"One moment," interrupted the astounded Colonel; "do you mean Hotchkiss the President of the Ditch Company?" He had recognized the name of a prominent citizen—a rigid, ascetic, taciturn, middle-aged man—a deacon—and more than that, the head of the company he had just defended. It seemed inconceivable.

"That's him," she continued, with eyes still fixed on the parasol and without changing her monotonous tone—"off and on ever since. Most of the time at the Free-Will Baptist

Church—at morning service, prayer-meetings, and such. And at home—outside—er—in the road."

"Is it this gentleman—Mr. Adoniram K. Hotchkiss—who—er—promised marriage?" stammered the Colonel.

"Yes."

The Colonel shifted uneasily in his chair. "Most extraordinary! for—you see—my dear young lady—this becomes—a—er—most delicate affair."

"That's what maw said," returned the young woman simply, yet with the faintest smile playing around her demure lips and downcast cheek.

"I mean," said the Colonel, with a pained yet courteous smile, "that this—er—gentleman—is in fact—er—one of my clients."

"That's what maw said too, and of course your knowing him will make it all the easier for you."

A slight flush crossed the Colonel's cheek as he returned quickly and a little stiffly, "On the contrary—er—it may make it impossible for me to—er—act in this matter."

The girl lifted her eyes. The Colonel held his breath as the long lashes were raised to his level. Even to an ordinary observer that sudden revelation of her eyes seemed to transform her face with subtle witchery. They were large, brown, and soft, yet filled with an extraordinary penetration and prescience. They were the eyes of an experienced woman of thirty fixed in the face of a child. What else the Colonel saw there Heaven only knows! He felt his inmost secrets plucked from him—his whole soul laid bare—his vanity, belligerency, gallantry—even his mediaeval chivalry, penetrated, and yet illuminated, in that single glance. And when the eyelids fell again, he felt that a greater part of himself had been swallowed up in them.

"I beg your pardon," he said hurriedly. "I mean—this matter may be arranged—er—amicably. My interest with—and as you wisely say—my—er—knowledge of my client—er—Mr. Hotchkiss—may effect—a compromise."

"And DAMAGES," said the young girl, readdressing her parasol, as if she had never looked up.

The Colonel winced. "And—er—undoubtedly COMPEN-SATION—if you do not press a fulfillment of the promise. Unless," he said, with an attempted return to his former easy gallantry, which, however, the recollection of her eyes made difficult, "it is a question of—er—the affections."

"Which?" asked his fair client softly.

"If you still love him?" explained the Colonel, actually blushing.

Zaidee again looked up; again taking the Colonel's breath away with eyes that expressed not only the fullest perception of what he had SAID, but of what he thought and had not said, and with an added subtle suggestion of what he might have thought. "That's tellin'," she said, dropping her long lashes again.

The Colonel laughed vacantly. Then feeling himself growing imbecile, he forced an equally weak gravity. "Pardon me—I understand there are no letters; may I know the way in which he formulated his declaration and promises?"

"Hymn-books."

"I beg your pardon," said the mystified lawyer.

"Hymn-books—marked words in them with pencil—and passed 'em on to me," repeated Zaidee. "Like 'love,' 'dear,' 'precious,' 'sweet,' and 'blessed,'" she added, accenting each word with a push of her parasol on the carpet. "Sometimes a whole line outer Tate and Brady—and Solomon's Song, you know, and sich."

"I believe," said the Colonel loftily, "that the—er—phrases of sacred psalmody lend themselves to the language of the affections. But in regard to the distinct promise of marriage —was there—er—no OTHER expression?"

"Marriage Service in the prayer-book—lines and words outer that—all marked," Zaidee replied.

The Colonel nodded naturally and approvingly. "Very good. Were others cognizant of this? Were there any witnesses?"

"Of course not," said the girl. "Only me and him. It was generally at church-time—or prayer-meeting. Once, in passing the plate, he slipped one o' them peppermint lozenges with the letters stamped on it 'I love you' for me to take."

The Colonel coughed slightly. "And you have the lozenge?"

"I ate it."

"Ah," said the Colonel. After a pause he added delicately, "But were these attentions—er—confined to—er—sacred precincts? Did he meet you elsewhere?"

"Useter pass our house on the road," returned the girl, dropping into her monotonous recital, "and useter signal."

"Ah, signal?" repeated the Colonel approvingly.

"Yes! He'd say 'Keerow,' and I'd say 'Keeree.' Suthing like a bird, you know."

Indeed, as she lifted her voice in imitation of the call, the Colonel thought it certainly very sweet and birdlike. At least as SHE gave it. With his remembrance of the grim deacon he had doubts as to the melodiousness of HIS utterance. He gravely made her repeat it.

"And after that signal?" he added suggestively.

"He'd pass on."

The Colonel again coughed slightly, and tapped his desk with his penholder.

"Were there any endearments—er—caresses—er—such as taking your hand—er—clasping your waist?" he suggested, with a gallant yet respectful sweep of his white hand and bowing of his head; "er—slight pressure of your fingers in the changes of a dance—I mean," he corrected himself, with an apologetic cough—"in the passing of the plate?"

"No; he was not what you'd call 'fond,'" returned the girl.

"Ah! Adoniram K. Hotchkiss was not 'fond' in the ordinary acceptance of the word," noted the Colonel, with professional gravity.

She lifted her disturbing eyes, and again absorbed his in her own. She also said "Yes," although her eyes in their mysterious prescience of all he was thinking disclaimed the necessity of any answer at all. He smiled vacantly. There was a long pause. On which she slowly disengaged her parasol from the carpet pattern, and stood up.

"I reckon that's about all," she said.

"Er—yes—but one moment," began the Colonel vaguely. He would have liked to keep her longer, but with her strange premonition of him he felt powerless to detain her, or explain his reason for doing so. He instinctively knew she had told him all; his professional judgment told him that a more hopeless case had never come to his knowledge. Yet he was not daunted, only embarrassed. "No matter," he said. "Of course I shall have to consult with you again."

Her eyes again answered that she expected he would, and she added simply, "When?"

"In the course of a day or two;" he replied quickly. "I will send you word."

She turned to go. In his eagerness to open the door for her, he upset his chair, and with some confusion, that was actually youthful, he almost impeded her movements in the hall, and knocked his broad-brimmed Panama hat from his bowing hand in a final gallant sweep. Yet as her small, trim, youthful figure, with its simple Leghorn straw hat confined by a blue bow under her round chin, passed away before him, she looked more like a child than ever.

The Colonel spent that afternoon in making diplomatic inquiries. He found his youthful client was the daughter of a widow who had a small ranch on the cross-roads, near the new Free-Will Baptist Church—the evident theatre of this pastoral. They led a secluded life, the girl being little known in the town, and her beauty and fascination apparently not yet being a recognized fact. The Colonel felt a pleasurable relief at this, and a general satisfaction he could not account for. His few inquiries concerning Mr. Hotchkiss only confirmed his own impressions of the alleged lover,—a serious-minded, practically abstracted man, abstentive of youthful society, and the last man apparently capable of levity of the affections or serious flirtation. The Colonel was mystified, but determined of purpose, whatever that purpose might have been.

The next day he was at his office at the same hour. He was alone—as usual—the Colonel's office being really his private lodgings, disposed in connecting rooms, a single apartment reserved for consultation. He had no clerk, his papers and briefs being taken by his faithful body-servant and ex-slave "Jim" to another firm who did his office work since the death of Major Stryker, the Colonel's only law partner, who fell in a duel some years previous. With a fine constancy the Colonel still retained his partner's name on his doorplate, and, it was alleged by the superstitious, kept a certain invincibility also through the 'manes' of that lamented and somewhat feared man.

The Colonel consulted his watch, whose heavy gold case still showed the marks of a providential interference with a bullet destined for its owner, and replaced it with some difficulty and shortness of breath in his fob. At the same moment he heard a step in the passage, and the door opened to Adoniram K. Hotchkiss. The Colonel was impressed; he had a duelist's respect for punctuality.

The man entered with a nod and the expectant inquiring look of a busy man. As his feet crossed that sacred threshold the Colonel became all courtesy; he placed a chair for his visitor, and took his hat from his half reluctant hand. He then opened a cupboard and brought out a bottle of whiskey and two glasses.

"A—er—slight refreshment, Mr. Hotchkiss," he suggested politely.

"I never drink," replied Hotchkiss, with the severe attitude of a total abstainer.

"Ah—er—not the finest Bourbon whiskey, selected by a Kentucky friend? No? Pardon me! A cigar, then—the mildest Havana."

"I do not use tobacco nor alcohol in any form," repeated Hotchkiss ascetically. "I have no foolish weaknesses."

The Colonel's moist, beady eyes swept silently over his client's sallow face. He leaned back comfortably in his chair, and half closing his eyes as in dreamy reminiscence, said slowly: "Your reply, Mr. Hotchkiss, reminds me of—er—sing'lar circumstance that—er—occurred, in point of fact—at the St. Charles Hotel, New Orleans. Pinkey Hornblower—personal friend—invited Senator Doolittle to join him in social glass. Received, sing'larly enough, reply similar to yours. 'Don't drink nor smoke?' said Pinkey. 'Gad, sir, you must be mighty sweet on the ladies.' Ha!" The Colonel paused long enough to allow the faint flush to pass from Hotchkiss's cheek, and went on, half closing his eyes: "'I allow no man, sir, to discuss my personal habits,' declared Doolittle, over his shirt collar. 'Then I reckon shootin' must be one of those habits,' said Pinkey coolly. Both men drove out on the Shell Road back of cemetery next morning. Pinkey put bullet at twelve paces through Doolittle's temple. Poor Doo never spoke again. Left three wives and seven children, they say—two of 'em black."

"I got a note from you this morning," said Hotchkiss, with badly concealed impatience. "I suppose in reference to our case. You have taken judgment, I believe."

The Colonel, without replying, slowly filled a glass of whiskey and water. For a moment he held it dreamily before him, as if still engaged in gentle reminiscences called up by the act. Then tossing it off, he wiped his lips with a large white handkerchief, and leaning back comfortably in his chair, said, with a wave of his hand, "The interview I requested, Mr. Hotchkiss, concerns a subject—which I may say is—er—er—at present NOT of a public or business nature—although LATER it might become—er—er—both. It is an affair of some—er—delicacy."

The Colonel paused, and Mr. Hotchkiss regarded him with increased impatience. The Colonel, however, continued, with unchanged deliberation: "It concerns—er—er—a young lady—a beautiful, high-souled creature, sir, who, apart from her personal loveliness—er—er—I may say is of one of the first families of Missouri, and—er—not remotely connected by marriage with one of—er—er—my boyhood's dearest friends." The latter, I grieve to say, was a pure invention of the Colonel's—an oratorical addition to the scanty information he had obtained the previous day. "The young lady," he continued blandly, "enjoys the further distinction of being the object of such attention from you as would make this interview—really—a confidential matter—er—er among friends and—er—er—relations in present and future. I need not say that the lady I refer to is Miss Zaidee Juno Hooker, only daughter of Almira Ann Hooker, relict of Jefferson Brown Hooker, formerly of Boone County, Kentucky, and latterly of—er—Pike County, Missouri."

The sallow, ascetic hue of Mr. Hotchkiss's face had passed through a livid and then a greenish shade, and finally settled into a sullen red. "What's all this about?" he demanded roughly.

The least touch of belligerent fire came into Starbottle's eye, but his bland courtesy did not change. "I believe," he said politely, "I have made myself clear as between—er—gentlemen, though perhaps not as clear as I should to—er—er—jury."

Mr. Hotchkiss was apparently struck with some significance in the lawyer's reply. "I don't know," he said, in a lower and more cautious voice, "what you mean by what you call 'my attentions' to—any one—or how it concerns you. I have not exchanged half a dozen words with—the person you name—have never written her a line—nor even called at her house."

He rose with an assumption of ease, pulled down his waistcoat, buttoned his coat, and took up his hat. The Colonel did not move.

"I believe I have already indicated my meaning in what I have called 'your attentions,'" said the Colonel blandly, "and given you my 'concern' for speaking as—er—er—mutual friend. As to YOUR statement of your relations with Miss Hooker, I may state that it is fully corroborated by the statement of the young lady herself in this very office yesterday."

"Then what does this impertinent nonsense mean? Why am I summoned here?" demanded Hotchkiss furiously.

"Because," said the Colonel deliberately, "that statement is infamously—yes, damnably to your discredit, sir!"

Mr. Hotchkiss was here seized by one of those impotent and inconsistent rages which occasionally betray the habitually cautious and timid man. He caught up the Colonel's stick, which was lying on the table. At the same moment the Colonel, without any apparent effort, grasped it by the handle. To Mr. Hotchkiss's astonishment, the stick separated in two pieces, leaving the handle and about two feet of narrow glittering steel in the Colonel's hand. The man recoiled, dropping the useless fragment. The Colonel picked it up, fitted the shining blade in it, clicked the spring, and then rising with a face of courtesy yet of unmistakably genuine pain, and with even a slight tremor in his voice, said gravely,—

"Mr. Hotchkiss, I owe you a thousand apologies, sir, that—er—a weapon should be drawn by me—even through your own inadvertence—under the sacred protection of my roof, and upon an unarmed man. I beg your pardon, sir, and I even withdraw the expressions which provoked that inadvertence. Nor does this apology prevent you from holding me responsible—personally responsible—ELSEWHERE for an indiscretion committed in behalf of a lady—my—er—client."

"Your client? Do you mean you have taken her case? You, the counsel for the Ditch Company?" asked Mr. Hotchkiss, in trembling indignation.

"Having won YOUR case, sir," replied the Colonel coolly, "the—er—usages of advocacy do not prevent me from espousing the cause of the weak and unprotected."

"We shall see, sir," said Hotchkiss, grasping the handle of the door and backing into the passage. "There are other lawyers who"—

"Permit me to see you out," interrupted the Colonel, rising politely.

—"will be ready to resist the attacks of blackmail," continued Hotchkiss, retreating along the passage.

"And then you will be able to repeat your remarks to me IN THE STREET," continued the Colonel, bowing, as he persisted in following his visitor to the door.

But here Mr. Hotchkiss quickly slammed it behind him, and hurried away. The Colonel returned to his office, and sitting down, took a sheet of letter-paper bearing the inscription "Starbottle and Stryker, Attorneys and Counselors," and wrote the following lines:—

HOOKER versus HOTCHKISS.

DEAR MADAM,—Having had a visit from the defendant in above, we should be pleased to have an interview with you at two P. M. to-morrow.

Your obedient servants,

STARBOTTLE AND STRYKER.

This he sealed and dispatched by his trusted servant Jim, and then devoted a few moments to reflection. It was the custom of the Colonel to act first, and justify the action by reason afterwards.

He knew that Hotchkiss would at once lay the matter before rival counsel. He knew that they would advise him that Miss Hooker had "no case"—that she would be nonsuited on her own evidence, and he ought not to compromise, but be ready to stand trial. He believed, however, that Hotchkiss feared such exposure, and although his own instincts had been at first against this remedy, he was now instinctively in favor of it. He remembered his own power with a jury; his vanity and his chivalry alike approved of this heroic method; he was bound by no prosaic facts—he had his own theory of the case, which no mere evidence could gainsay. In fact, Mrs. Hooker's admission that he was to "tell the story in his own way" actually appeared to him an inspiration and a prophecy.

Perhaps there was something else, due possibly to the lady's wonderful eyes, of which he had thought much. Yet it was not her simplicity that affected him solely; on the contrary, it was her apparent intelligent reading of the character of her recreant lover—and of his own! Of all the Colonel's previous "light" or "serious" loves, none had ever before flattered him in that way. And it was this, combined with the respect which he had held for their professional relations, that precluded his having a more familiar knowledge of his client, through serious questioning or playful gallantry. I am not sure it was not part of the charm to have a rustic femme incomprise as a client.

Nothing could exceed the respect with which he greeted her as she entered his office the next day. He even affected not to notice that she had put on her best clothes, and he made no doubt appeared as when she had first attracted the mature yet faithless attentions of Deacon Hotchkiss at church. A white virginal muslin was belted around her slim figure by a blue ribbon, and her Leghorn hat was drawn around her oval cheek by a bow of the same color. She had a Southern girl's narrow feet, encased in white stockings and kid slippers, which were crossed primly before her as she sat in a chair, supporting her arm by her faithful parasol planted firmly on the floor. A faint odor of southernwood exhaled from her, and, oddly enough, stirred the Colonel with a far-off recollection of a pine-shaded Sunday-school on a Georgia hillside, and of his first love, aged ten, in a short starched frock. Possibly it was the same recollection that revived something of the awkwardness he had felt then.

He, however, smiled vaguely, and sitting down, coughed slightly, and placed his finger-tips together. "I have had an—er—interview with Mr. Hotchkiss, but—I—er—regret to say there seems to be no prospect of—er—compromise."

He paused, and to his surprise her listless "company" face lit up with an adorable smile. "Of course!—ketch him!" she said. "Was he mad when you told him?" She put her knees comfortably together and leaned forward for a reply.

For all that, wild horses could not have torn from the Colonel a word about Hotchkiss's anger. "He expressed his intention of employing counsel—and defending a suit," returned the Colonel, affably basking in her smile.

She dragged her chair nearer his desk. "Then you'll fight him tooth and nail?" she asked eagerly; "you'll show him up? You'll tell the whole story your own way? You'll give him fits?—and you'll make him pay? Sure?" she went on breathlessly.

"I—er—will," said the Colonel, almost as breathlessly.

She caught his fat white hand, which was lying on the table, between her own and lifted it to her lips. He felt her soft young fingers even through the lisle-thread gloves that encased them, and the warm moisture of her lips upon his skin. He felt himself flushing—but was unable to break the silence or change his position. The next moment she had scuttled back with her chair to her old position.

"I—er—certainly shall do my best," stammered the Colonel, in an attempt to recover his dignity and composure.

"That's enough! You'll do it," said she enthusiastically. "Lordy! Just you talk for ME as ye did for HIS old Ditch

Company, and you'll fetch it—every time! Why, when you made that jury sit up the other day—when you got that off about the Merrikan flag waving equally over the rights of honest citizens banded together in peaceful commercial pursuits, as well as over the fortress of official proflig—"

"Oligarchy," murmured the Colonel courteously.

—"oligarchy," repeated the girl quickly, "my breath was just took away. I said to maw, 'Ain't he too sweet for anything!' I did, honest Injin! And when you rolled it all off at the end—never missing a word (you didn't need to mark 'em in a lesson-book, but had 'em all ready on your tongue)—and walked out—Well! I didn't know you nor the Ditch Company from Adam, but I could have just run over and kissed you there before the whole court!"

She laughed, with her face glowing, although her strange eyes were cast down. Alack! the Colonel's face was equally flushed, and his own beady eyes were on his desk. To any other woman he would have voiced the banal gallantry that he should now, himself, look forward to that reward, but the words never reached his lips. He laughed, coughed slightly, and when he looked up again she had fallen into the same attitude as on her first visit, with her parasol point on the floor.

"I must ask you to—er—direct your memory to—er—another point: the breaking off of the—er—er—er—engagement. Did he—er—give any reason for it? Or show any cause?"

"No; he never said anything," returned the girl.

"Not in his usual way?—er—no reproaches out of the hymn-book?—or the sacred writings?"

Bret Harte

"No; he just QUIT."

"Er—ceased his attentions," said the Colonel gravely. "And naturally you—er—were not conscious of any cause for his doing so."

The girl raised her wonderful eyes so suddenly and so penetratingly without replying in any other way that the Colonel could only hurriedly say: "I see! None, of course!"

At which she rose, the Colonel rising also. "We—shall begin proceedings at once. I must, however, caution you to answer no questions, nor say anything about this case to any one until you are in court."

She answered his request with another intelligent look and a nod. He accompanied her to the door. As he took her proffered hand, he raised the lisle-thread fingers to his lips with old-fashioned gallantry. As if that act had condoned for his first omissions and awkwardness, he became his old-fashioned self again, buttoned his coat, pulled out his shirt frill, and strutted back to his desk.

A day or two later it was known throughout the town that Zaidee Hooker had sued Adoniram Hotchkiss for breach of promise, and that the damages were laid at five thousand dollars. As in those bucolic days the Western press was under the secure censorship of a revolver, a cautious tone of criticism prevailed, and any gossip was confined to personal expression, and even then at the risk of the gossiper. Nevertheless, the situation provoked the intensest curiosity. The Colonel was approached—until his statement that he should consider any attempt to overcome his professional secrecy a personal reflection withheld further advances. The community were left to the more ostentatious information of the defendant's counsel, Messrs. Kitcham and Bilser, that the case was "ridiculous" and "rotten," that the plaintiff would be nonsuited, and the fire-eating Starbottle would be taught a lesson that he could not "bully" the law, and there were some dark hints of a conspiracy. It was even hinted that the "case" was the revengeful and preposterous outcome of the refusal of Hotchkiss to pay Starbottle an extravagant fee for his late services to the Ditch Company. It is unnecessary to say that these words were not reported to the Colonel. It was, however, an unfortunate circumstance for the calmer, ethical consideration of the subject that the Church sided with Hotchkiss, as this provoked an equal adherence to the plaintiff and Starbottle on the part of the larger body of non-churchgoers, who were delighted at a possible exposure of the weakness of religious rectitude. "I've allus had my suspicions o' them early candle-light meetings down at that gospel shop," said one critic, "and I reckon Deacon Hotchkiss didn't rope in the gals to attend jest for psalm-singing." "Then for him to get up and leave the board afore the game's finished and try to sneak out of it," said an other,—"I suppose that's what they call RELIGIOUS."

It was therefore not remarkable that the court-house three weeks later was crowded with an excited multitude of the curious and sympathizing. The fair plaintiff, with her mother, was early in attendance, and under the Colonel's advice appeared in the same modest garb in which she had first visited his office. This and her downcast, modest demeanor were perhaps at first disappointing to the crowd, who had evidently expected a paragon of loveliness in this Circe of that grim, ascetic defendant, who sat beside his counsel. But presently all eyes were fixed on the Colonel, who certainly made up in his appearance any deficiency of his fair client. His portly figure was clothed in a blue dress coat with brass buttons, a buff waistcoat which permitted his frilled shirt-front to become erectile above it, a black satin stock which confined a boyish turned-down collar around his full neck, and immaculate drill trousers, strapped over varnished boots. A murmur ran round the court. "Old 'Personally Responsible' has got his war-paint on;" "The Old War-Horse is smelling powder," were whispered comments. Yet for all that, the most irreverent among them recognized vaguely, in this bizarre figure, something of an honored past in their country's history, and possibly felt the spell of old deeds and old names that had once thrilled their boyish pulses. The new District Judge returned Colonel Starbottle's profoundly punctilious bow. The Colonel was followed by his negro servant, carrying a parcel of hymn-books and Bibles, who, with a courtesy evidently imitated from his master, placed one before the opposite counsel. This, after a first curious glance, the lawyer somewhat superciliously tossed aside. But when Jim, proceeding to the jury-box, placed with equal politeness the remaining copies before the jury, the opposite counsel sprang to his feet.

"I want to direct the attention of the Court to this unprecedented tampering with the jury, by this gratuitous exhibition of matter impertinent and irrelevant to the issue."

The Judge cast an inquiring look at Colonel Starbottle.

"May it please the Court," returned Colonel Starbottle with dignity, ignoring the counsel, "the defendant's counsel will observe that he is already furnished with the matter—which I regret to say he has treated—in the presence of the Court— and of his client, a deacon of the church—with—er—great superciliousness. When I state to your Honor that the books in question are hymn-books and copies of the Holy Scriptures, and that they are for the instruction of the jury, to whom I shall have to refer them in the course of my opening, I believe I am within my rights."

"The act is certainly unprecedented," said the Judge dryly,

"but unless the counsel for the plaintiff expects the jury to SING from these hymn-books, their introduction is not improper, and I cannot admit the objection. As defendant's counsel are furnished with copies also, they cannot plead 'surprise,' as in the introduction of new matter, and as plaintiff's counsel relies evidently upon the jury's attention to his opening, he would not be the first person to distract it." After a pause he added, addressing the Colonel, who remained standing, "The Court is with you, sir; proceed."

But the Colonel remained motionless and statuesque, with folded arms.

"I have overruled the objection," repeated the Judge; "you may go on."

"I am waiting, your Honor, for the—er—withdrawal by the defendant's counsel of the word 'tampering,' as refers to myself, and of 'impertinent,' as refers to the sacred volumes."

"The request is a proper one, and I have no doubt will be acceded to," returned the Judge quietly. The defendant's counsel rose and mumbled a few words of apology, and the incident closed. There was, however, a general feeling that the Colonel had in some way "scored," and if his object had been to excite the greatest curiosity about the books, he had made his point.

But impassive of his victory, he inflated his chest, with his right hand in the breast of his buttoned coat, and began. His usual high color had paled slightly, but the small pupils of his prominent eyes glittered like steel. The young girl leaned forward in her chair with an attention so breathless, a sympathy so quick, and an admiration so artless and unconscious that in an instant she divided with the speaker the attention of the whole assemblage. It was very hot; the court was crowded to suffocation; even the open windows revealed a crowd of faces outside the building, eagerly following the Colonel's words.

He would remind the jury that only a few weeks ago he stood there as the advocate of a powerful Company, then represented by the present defendant. He spoke then as the champion of strict justice against legal oppression; no less should he to-day champion the cause of the unprotected and the comparatively defenseless—save for that paramount power which surrounds beauty and innocence—even though the plaintiff of yesterday was the defendant of to-day. As he approached the court a moment ago he had raised his eyes and beheld the starry flag flying from its dome, and he knew that glorious banner was a symbol of the perfect equality, under the Constitution, of the rich and the poor, the strong and the weak—an equality which made the simple citizen taken from the plough in the field, the pick in the gulch, or from behind the counter in the mining town, who served on that jury, the equal arbiters of justice with that highest legal luminary whom they were proud to welcome on the bench to-day. The Colonel paused, with a stately bow to the impassive Judge. It was this, he continued, which lifted his heart as he approached the building. And yet—he had entered it with an uncertain—he might almost say—a timid step. And why? He knew, gentlemen, he was about to confront a profound—aye! a sacred responsibility! Those hymn-books and holy writings handed to the jury were NOT, as his Honor had surmised, for the purpose of enabling the jury to indulge in—er—preliminary choral exercise! He might, indeed, say, "Alas, not!" They were the damning, incontrovertible proofs of the perfidy of the defendant. And they would prove as terrible a warning to him as the fatal characters upon Belshazzar's wall. There was a strong sensation. Hotchkiss turned a sallow green. His lawyers assumed a careless smile.

It was his duty to tell them that this was not one of those ordinary "breach-of-promise" cases which were too often the occasion of ruthless mirth and indecent levity in the court-room. The jury would find nothing of that here. There were no love-letters with the epithets of endearment, nor those mystic crosses and ciphers which, he had been credibly informed, chastely hid the exchange of those mutual caresses known as "kisses." There was no cruel tearing of the veil from those sacred privacies of the human affection; there was no forensic shouting out of those fond confidences meant only for ONE. But there was, he was shocked to say, a new sacrilegious intrusion. The weak pipings of Cupid were mingled with the chorus of the saints,—the sanctity of the temple known as the "meeting—house" was desecrated by proceedings more in keeping with the shrine of Venus; and the inspired writings themselves were used as the medium of amatory and wanton flirtation by the defendant in his sacred capacity as deacon.

The Colonel artistically paused after this thunderous denunciation. The jury turned eagerly to the leaves of the hymn-books, but the larger gaze of the audience remained fixed upon the speaker and the girl, who sat in rapt admiration of his periods. After the hush, the Colonel continued in a lower and sadder voice: "There are, perhaps, few of us here, gentlemen,—with the exception of the defendant,—who can arrogate to themselves the title of regular church-goers, or to whom these humbler functions of the prayer-meeting, the Sunday-school, and the Bible-class are habitually familiar. Yet"—more solemnly—"down in our hearts is the deep conviction of our shortcomings and failings, and a laudable desire that others, at least, should profit by the teachings we neglect. Perhaps," he continued, closing his eyes dreamily, "there is not a man here who does not recall the happy days of his boyhood, the rustic village spire, the lessons shared with some artless village maiden, with whom he later sauntered, hand in hand, through the woods, as the simple rhyme rose upon their lips,—

'Always make it a point to have it a rule,
Never to be late at the Sabbath-school.'

"He would recall the strawberry feasts, the welcome annual picnic, redolent with hunks of gingerbread and sarsaparilla. How would they feel to know that these sacred recollections were now forever profaned in their memory by the knowledge that the defendant was capable of using such occasions to make love to the larger girls and teachers, whilst his artless companions were innocently—the Court will pardon me for introducing what I am credibly informed is the local expression—'doing gooseberry'?" The tremulous flicker of a smile passed over the faces of the listening crowd, and the Colonel slightly winced. But he recovered himself instantly, and continued,—

"My client, the only daughter of a widowed mother—who has for years stemmed the varying tides of adversity, in the western precincts of this town—stands before you to-day invested only in her own innocence. She wears no—er—rich gifts of her faithless admirer—is panoplied in no jewels, rings, nor mementos of affection such as lovers delight to hang upon the shrine of their affections; hers is not the glory with which Solomon decorated the Queen of Sheba, though the defendant, as I shall show later, clothed her in the less expensive flowers of the king's poetry. No, gentlemen! The defendant exhibited in this affair a certain frugality of—er—pecuniary investment, which I am willing to admit may be commendable in his class. His only gift was characteristic alike of his methods and his economy. There is, I understand, a certain not unimportant feature of religious exercise known as 'taking a collection.' The defendant, on this occasion, by the mute presentation of a tin plate covered with baize, solicited the pecuniary contributions of the faithful. On approaching the plaintiff, however, he himself slipped a love-token upon the plate and pushed it towards her. That love-token was a lozenge—a small disk, I have reason to believe, concocted of peppermint and sugar, bearing upon its reverse surface the simple words, 'I love you!' I have since ascertained that these disks may be bought for five cents a dozen—or at considerably less than one half cent for the single lozenge. Yes, gentlemen, the words 'I love you!'—the oldest legend of all; the refrain 'when the morning stars sang together'—were presented to the plaintiff by a medium so insignificant that there is, happily, no coin in the republic low enough to represent its value.

"I shall prove to you, gentlemen of the jury," said the Colonel solemnly, drawing a Bible from his coat-tail pocket, "that the defendant for the last twelve months conducted an amatory correspondence with the plaintiff by means of underlined words of Sacred Writ and church psalmody, such as 'beloved,' 'precious,' and 'dearest,' occasionally appropriating whole passages which seemed apposite to his tender passion. I shall call your attention to one of them. The defendant, while professing to be a total abstainer,—a man who, in my own knowledge, has refused spirituous refreshment as an inordinate weakness of the flesh,—with shameless hypocrisy underscores with his pencil the following passage, and presents it to the plaintiff. The gentlemen of the jury will find it in the Song of Solomon, page 548, chapter ii. verse 5." After a pause, in which the rapid rustling of leaves was heard in the jury-box, Colonel Starbottle declaimed in a pleading, stentorian voice, "'Stay me with—er—FLAGONS, comfort me with—er—apples—for I am—er—sick of love.' Yes, gentlemen!—yes, you may well turn from those accusing pages and look at the double-faced defendant. He desires—to—er—be—'stayed with flagons'! I am not aware at present what kind of liquor is habitually dispensed at these meetings, and for which the defendant so urgently clamored; but it will be my duty, before this trial is over, to discover it, if I have to summon every barkeeper in this district. For the moment I will simply call your attention to the QUANTITY. It is not a single drink that the defendant asks for—not a glass of light and generous wine, to be shared with his inamorata, but a number of flagons or vessels, each possibly holding a pint measure— FOR HIMSELF!"

The smile of the audience had become a laugh. The Judge looked up warningly, when his eye caught the fact that the Colonel had again winced at this mirth. He regarded him seriously. Mr. Hotchkiss's counsel had joined in the laugh affectedly, but Hotchkiss himself sat ashy pale. There was also a commotion in the jury-box, a hurried turning over of leaves, and an excited discussion.

"The gentlemen of the jury," said the Judge, with official gravity, "will please keep order and attend only to the speeches of counsel. Any discussion HERE is irregular and premature, and must be reserved for the jury-room after they have retired."

The foreman of the jury struggled to his feet. He was a powerful man, with a good-humored face, and, in spite of his unfelicitous nickname of "The Bone-Breaker," had a kindly, simple, but somewhat emotional nature. Nevertheless, it appeared as if he were laboring under some powerful indignation.

"Can we ask a question, Judge?" he said respectfully, although his voice had the unmistakable Western American ring in it, as of one who was unconscious that he could be addressing any but his peers.

"Yes," said the Judge good-humoredly.

"We're finding in this yere piece, out o' which the Kernel hes just bin a-quotin', some language that me and my pardners allow hadn't orter be read out afore a young lady in court, and we want to know of you—ez a fa'r-minded and impartial man—ef this is the reg'lar kind o' book given to gals and babies down at the meetin'-house."

"The jury will please follow the counsel's speech without comment," said the Judge briefly, fully aware that the defendant's counsel would spring to his feet, as he did promptly.

"The Court will allow us to explain to the gentlemen that the language they seem to object to has been accepted by the best theologians for the last thousand years as being purely mystic. As I will explain later, those are merely symbols of the Church"—

"Of wot?" interrupted the foreman, in deep scorn.

"Of the Church!"

"We ain't askin' any questions o' YOU, and we ain't takin' any answers," said the foreman, sitting down abruptly.

"I must insist," said the Judge sternly, "that the plaintiff's counsel be allowed to continue his opening without interruption. You" (to defendant's counsel) "will have your opportunity to reply later."

The counsel sank down in his seat with the bitter conviction that the jury was manifestly against him, and the case as good as lost. But his face was scarcely as disturbed as his client's, who, in great agitation, had begun to argue with him wildly, and was apparently pressing some point against the lawyer's vehement opposal. The Colonel's murky eyes brightened as he still stood erect, with his hand thrust in his breast.

"It will be put to you, gentlemen, when the counsel on the other side refrains from mere interruption and confines himself to reply, that my unfortunate client has no action— no remedy at law—because there were no spoken words of endearment. But, gentlemen, it will depend upon YOU to say what are and what are not articulate expressions of love. We all know that among the lower animals, with whom you may possibly be called upon to classify the defendant, there are certain signals more or less harmonious, as the case may be. The ass brays, the horse neighs, the sheep bleats—the feathered denizens of the grove call to their mates in more musical roundelays. These are recognized facts, gentlemen, which you yourselves, as dwellers among nature in this beautiful land, are all cognizant of. They are facts that no one would deny—and we should have a poor opinion of the ass who, at—er—such a supreme moment, would attempt to suggest that his call was unthinking and without significance. But, gentlemen, I shall prove to you that such was the foolish, self-convicting custom of the defendant. With the greatest reluctance, and the—er—greatest pain, I succeeded in wresting from the maidenly modesty of my fair client the innocent confession that the defendant had induced her to correspond with him in these methods. Picture to yourself, gentlemen, the lonely moonlight road beside the widow's humble cottage. It is a beautiful night, sanctified to the affections, and the innocent girl is leaning from her casement. Presently there appears upon the road a slinking, stealthy figure, the defendant on his way to church. True to the instruction she has received from him, her lips part in the musical utterance" (the Colonel lowered his voice in a faint falsetto, presumably in fond imitation of his fair client),

"'Keeree!' Instantly the night becomes resonant with the impassioned reply" (the Colonel here lifted his voice in stentorian tones), "'Kee-row.' Again, as he passes, rises the soft 'Keeree;' again, as his form is lost in the distance, comes back the deep 'Keerow.'"

A burst of laughter, long, loud, and irrepressible, struck the whole court-room, and before the Judge could lift his half-composed face and take his handkerchief from his mouth, a faint "Keeree" from some unrecognized obscurity of the court-room was followed by a loud "Keerow" from some opposite locality. "The Sheriff will clear the court," said the Judge sternly; but, alas! as the embarrassed and choking officials rushed hither and thither, a soft "Keeree" from the spectators at the window, OUTSIDE the court-house, was answered by a loud chorus of "Keerows" from the opposite windows, filled with onlookers. Again the laughter arose everywhere,—even the fair plaintiff herself sat convulsed behind her handkerchief.

The figure of Colonel Starbottle alone remained erect— white and rigid. And then the Judge, looking up, saw—what no one else in the court had seen—that the Colonel was sincere and in earnest; that what he had conceived to be the pleader's most perfect acting and most elaborate irony were the deep, serious, mirthless CONVICTIONS of a man without the least sense of humor. There was the respect of this conviction in the Judge's voice as he said to him gently, "You may proceed, Colonel Starbottle."

"I thank your Honor," said the Colonel slowly, "for recognizing and doing all in your power to prevent an interruption that, during my thirty years' experience at the bar, I have never been subjected to without the privilege of holding the instigators thereof responsible—PERSONALLY responsible. It is possibly my fault that I have failed, oratorically, to convey to the gentlemen of the jury the full force and significance of the defendant's signals. I am aware that my voice is singularly deficient in producing either the dulcet tones of my fair client or the impassioned vehemence of the defendant's response. I will," continued the Colonel, with a fatigued but blind fatuity that ignored the hurriedly knit brows and warning eyes of the Judge, "try again. The note uttered by my client" (lowering his voice to the faintest of falsettos) "was 'Keeree;' the response was 'Keerow-ow.'" And the Colonel's voice fairly shook the dome above him.

Another uproar of laughter followed this apparently audacious repetition, but was interrupted by an unlooked-for incident. The defendant rose abruptly, and tearing himself away from the withholding hand and pleading protestations of his counsel, absolutely fled from the court-room, his appearance outside being recognized by a prolonged "Keerow" from the bystanders, which again and again followed him in the distance.

In the momentary silence which followed, the Colonel's voice was heard saying, "We rest here, your Honor," and he sat down. No less white, but more agitated, was the face of the defendant's counsel, who instantly rose.

"For some unexplained reason, your Honor, my client desires to suspend further proceedings, with a view to effect a peaceable compromise with the plaintiff. As he is a man of wealth and position, he is able and willing to pay liberally for that privilege. While I, as his counsel, am still convinced of his legal irresponsibility, as he has chosen publicly to abandon his rights here, I can only ask your Honor's permission to suspend further proceedings until I can confer with Colonel Starbottle."

"As far as I can follow the pleadings," said the Judge

gravely, "the case seems to be hardly one for litigation, and I approve of the defendant's course, while I strongly urge the plaintiff to accept it."

Colonel Starbottle bent over his fair client. Presently he rose, unchanged in look or demeanor. "I yield, your Honor, to the wishes of my client, and—er—lady. We accept."

Before the court adjourned that day it was known throughout the town that Adoniram K. Hotchkiss had compromised the suit for four thousand dollars and costs.

Colonel Starbottle had so far recovered his equanimity as to strut jauntily towards his office, where he was to meet his fair client. He was surprised, however, to find her already there, and in company with a somewhat sheepish-looking young man—a stranger. If the Colonel had any disappointment in meeting a third party to the interview, his old-fashioned courtesy did not permit him to show it. He bowed graciously, and politely motioned them each to a seat.

"I reckoned I'd bring Hiram round with me," said the young lady, lifting her searching eyes, after a pause, to the Colonel's, "though he WAS awful shy, and allowed that you didn't know him from Adam, or even suspect his existence. But I said, 'That's just where you slip up, Hiram; a pow'ful man like the Colonel knows everything—and I've seen it in his eye.' Lordy!" she continued, with a laugh, leaning forward over her parasol, as her eyes again sought the Colonel's, "don't you remember when you asked me if I loved that old Hotchkiss, and I told you, 'That's tellin',' and you looked at me—Lordy! I knew THEN you suspected there was a Hiram SOMEWHERE, as good as if I'd told you. Now you jest get up, Hiram, and give the Colonel a good hand-shake. For if it wasn't for HIM and HIS searchin' ways, and HIS awful power of language, I wouldn't hev got that four thousand dollars out o' that flirty fool Hotchkiss—enough to buy a farm, so as you and me could get married! That's what you owe to HIM. Don't stand there like a stuck fool starin' at him. He won't eat you—though he's killed many a better man. Come, have I got to do ALL the kissin'?"

It is of record that the Colonel bowed so courteously and so profoundly that he managed not merely to evade the proffered hand of the shy Hiram, but to only lightly touch the franker and more impulsive finger-tips of the gentle Zaidee. "I—er—offer my sincerest congratulations—though I think you—er—overestimate—my—er—powers of penetration. Unfortunately, a pressing engagement, which may oblige me also to leave town tonight, forbids my saying more. I have—er—left the—er—business settlement of this—er—case in the hands of the lawyers who do my office work, and who will show you every attention. And now let me wish you a very good afternoon."

Nevertheless, the Colonel returned to his private room, and it was nearly twilight when the faithful Jim entered, to find him sitting meditatively before his desk. "'Fo' God! Kernel, I hope dey ain't nuffin de matter, but you's lookin' mighty solemn! I ain't seen you look dat way, Kernel, since de day pooh Massa Stryker was fetched home shot froo de head."

"Hand me down the whiskey, Jim," said the Colonel, rising slowly.

The negro flew to the closet joyfully, and brought out the bottle. The Colonel poured out a glass of the spirit and drank it with his old deliberation.

"You're quite right, Jim," he said, putting down his glass, "but I'm—er—getting old—and—somehow I am missing poor Stryker damnably!"

THE LANDLORD OF THE BIG FLUME HOTEL

The Big Flume stage-coach had just drawn up at the Big Flume Hotel simultaneously with the ringing of a large dinner bell in the two hands of a negro waiter, who, by certain gyrations of the bell was trying to impart to his performance that picturesque elegance and harmony which the instrument and its purpose lacked. For the refreshment thus proclaimed was only the ordinary station dinner, protracted at Big Flume for three quarters of an hour, to allow for the arrival of the connecting mail from Sacramento, although the repast was of a nature that seldom prevailed upon the traveler to linger the full period over its details. The ordinary cravings of hunger were generally satisfied in half an hour, and the remaining minutes were employed by the passengers in drowning the memory of their meal in "drinks at the bar," in smoking, and even in a hurried game of "old sledge," or dominoes. Yet to-day the deserted table was still occupied by a belated traveler, and a lady—separated by a wilderness of empty dishes—who had arrived after the stage-coach. Observing which, the landlord, perhaps touched by this unwonted appreciation of his fare, moved forward to give them his personal attention.

He was a man, however, who seemed to be singularly deficient in those supreme qualities which in the West have exalted the ability to "keep a hotel" into a proverbial synonym for superexcellence. He had little or no innovating genius, no trade devices, no assumption, no faculty for advertisement, no progressiveness, and no "racket." He had the tolerant good-humor of the Southwestern pioneer, to whom cyclones, famine, drought, floods, pestilence, and savages were things to be accepted, and whom disaster, if it did not stimulate, certainly did not appall. He received the insults, complaints, and criticisms of hurried and hungry passengers, the comments and threats of the Stage Company as he had submitted to the aggressions of a stupid, unjust, but overruling Nature—with unshaken calm. Perhaps herein lay his strength. People were obliged to submit to him and his hotel as part of the unfinished civilization, and they even saw something humorous in his impassiveness. Those who preferred to remonstrate with him emerged from the discussion with the general feeling of having been played with by a large-hearted and paternally disposed bear. Tall and long-limbed, with much strength in his lazy muscles, there was also a prevailing impression that this feeling might be intensified if the discussion were ever carried to physical contention. Of his personal history it was known only that he had emigrated from Wisconsin in 1852, that he had calmly unyoked his ox teams at Big Flume, then a trackless wilderness, and on the opening of a wagon road to the new mines had built a wayside station which eventually developed into the present hotel. He had been divorced in a Western State by his wife "Rosalie," locally known as "The Prairie Flower of Elkham Creek," for incompatibility of temper! Her temper was not stated.

Such was Abner Langworthy, the proprietor, as he moved leisurely down towards the lady guest, who was nearest, and who was sitting with her back to the passage between the tables. Stopping, occasionally, to professionally adjust the tablecloths and glasses, he at last reached her side.

"Ef there's anythin' more ye want that ye ain't seein', ma'am," he began—and stopped suddenly. For the lady had looked up at the sound of his voice. It was his divorced wife, whom he had not seen since their separation. The recognition was instantaneous, mutual, and characterized by perfect equanimity on both sides.

"Well! I wanter know!" said the lady, although the exclamation point was purely conventional. "Abner Langworthy! though perhaps I've no call to say 'Abner.'"

"Same to you, Rosalie—though I say it too," returned the landlord. "But hol' on just a minit." He moved forward to the other guest, put the same perfunctory question regarding his needs, received a negative answer, and then returned to the lady and dropped into a chair opposite to her.

"You're looking peart and—fleshy," he said resignedly, as if he were tolerating his own conventional politeness with his other difficulties; "unless," he added cautiously, "you're takin' on some new disease."

"No! I'm fairly comf'ble," responded the lady calmly, "and you're gettin' on in the vale, ez is natural—though you still kind o' run to bone, as you used."

There was not a trace of malevolence in either of their comments, only a resigned recognition of certain unpleasant truths which seemed to have been habitual to both of them. Mr. Langworthy paused to flick away some flies from the butter with his professional napkin, and resumed,—

"It must be a matter o' five years sens I last saw ye, isn't it?— in court arter you got the decree—you remember?"

"Yes—the 28th o' July, '51. I paid Lawyer Hoskins's bill that very day—that's how I remember," returned the lady. "You've got a big business here," she continued, glancing round the room; "I reckon you're makin' it pay. Don't seem to be in your line, though; but then, thar wasn't many things that was."

"No—that's so," responded Mr. Langworthy, nodding his head, as assenting to an undeniable proposition, "and you—I suppose you're gettin' on too. I reckon you're—er—married —eh?"—with a slight suggestion of putting the question delicately.

The lady nodded, ignoring the hesitation. "Yes, let me see, it's just three years and three days. Constantine Byers—I don't reckon you know him—from Milwaukee. Timber merchant. Standin' timber's his specialty."

"And I reckon he's—satisfactory?"

"Yes! Mr. Byers is a good provider—and handy. And you? I should say you'd want a wife in this business?"

Mr. Langworthy's serious half-perfunctory manner here took on an appearance of interest. "Yes—I've bin thinkin' that way. Thar's a young woman helpin' in the kitchen ez might do, though I'm not certain, and I ain't lettin' on anything as yet. You might take a look at her, Rosalie,—I orter say Mrs. Byers ez is,—and kinder size her up, and gimme the result. It's still wantin' seven minutes o' schedule time afore the stage goes, and—if you ain't wantin' more food"—delicately, as became a landlord—"and ain't got anythin' else to do, it might pass the time."

Strange as it may seem, Mrs. Byers here displayed an equal animation in her fresh face as she rose promptly to her feet and began to rearrange her dust cloak around her buxom figure. "I don't mind, Abner," she said, "and I don't think that Mr. Byers would mind either;" then seeing Langworthy hesitating at the latter unexpected suggestion, she added confidently, "and I wouldn't mind even if he did, for I'm sure if I don't know the kind o' woman you'd be likely to need, I don't know who would. Only last week I was sayin' like that to Mr. Byers"—

"To Mr. Byers?" said Abner, with some surprise.

"Yes—to him. I said, 'We've been married three years, Constantine, and ef I don't know by this time what kind o' woman you need now—and might need in future—why, thar ain't much use in matrimony.'"

"You was always wise, Rosalie," said Abner, with reminiscent appreciation.

"I was always there, Abner," returned Mrs. Byers, with a complacent show of dimples, which she, however, chastened into that resignation which seemed characteristic of the pair. "Let's see your 'intended'—as might be."

Thus supported, Mr. Langworthy led Mrs. Byers into the hall through a crowd of loungers, into a smaller hall, and there opened the door of the kitchen. It was a large room, whose windows were half darkened by the encompassing pines which still pressed around the house on the scantily cleared site. A number of men and women, among them a Chinaman and a negro, were engaged in washing dishes and other culinary duties; and beside the window stood a young blonde girl, who was wiping a tin pan which she was also using to hide a burst of laughter evidently caused by the abrupt entrance of her employer. A quantity of fluffy hair and part of a white, bared arm were nevertheless visible outside the disk, and Mrs. Byers gathered from the direction of Mr.

Langworthy's eyes, assisted by a slight nudge from his elbow, that this was the selected fair one. His feeble explanatory introduction, addressed to the occupants generally, "Just showing the house to Mrs.—er—Dusenberry," convinced her that the circumstances of his having been divorced he had not yet confided to the young woman. As he turned almost immediately away, Mrs. Byers in following him managed to get a better look at the girl, as she was exchanging some facetious remark to a neighbor. Mr. Langworthy did not speak until they had reached the deserted dining-room again.

"Well?" he said briefly, glancing at the clock, "what did ye think o' Mary Ellen?"

To any ordinary observer the girl in question would have seemed the least fitted in age, sobriety of deportment, and administrative capacity to fill the situation thus proposed for her, but Mrs. Byers was not an ordinary observer, and her auditor was not an ordinary listener.

"She's older than she gives herself out to be," said Mrs. Byers tentatively, "and them kitten ways don't amount to much."

Mr. Langworthy nodded. Had Mrs. Byers discovered a homicidal tendency in Mary Ellen he would have been equally unmoved.

"She don't handsome much," continued Mrs. Byers musingly, "but"—

"I never was keen on good looks in a woman, Rosalie. You know that!" Mrs. Byers received the equivocal remark unemotionally, and returned to the subject.

"Well!" she said contemplatively, "I should think you could

make her suit."

Mr. Langworthy nodded with resigned toleration of all that might have influenced her judgment and his own. "I was wantin' a fa'r-minded opinion, Rosalie, and you happened along jest in time. Kin I put up anythin' in the way of food for ye?" he added, as a stir outside and the words "All aboard!" proclaimed the departing of the stage-coach,—"an orange or a hunk o' gingerbread, freshly baked?"

"Thank ye kindly, Abner, but I sha'n't be usin' anythin' afore supper," responded Mrs. Byers, as they passed out into the veranda beside the waiting coach.

Mr. Langworthy helped her to her seat. "Ef you're passin' this way ag'in"—he hesitated delicately.

"I'll drop in, or I reckon Mr. Byers might, he havin' business along the road," returned Mrs. Byers with a cheerful nod, as the coach rolled away and the landlord of the Big Flume Hotel reentered his house.

For the next three weeks, however, it did not appear that Mr. Langworthy was in any hurry to act upon the advice of his former wife. His relations to Mary Ellen Budd were characterized by his usual tolerance to his employees' failings,—which in Mary Ellen's case included many "breakages,"—but were not marked by the invasion of any warmer feeling, or a desire for confidences. The only perceptible divergence from his regular habits was a disposition to be on the veranda at the arrival of the stage-coach, and when his duties permitted this, a cautious survey of his female guests at the beginning of dinner. This probably led to his more or less ignoring any peculiarities in his masculine patrons or their claims to his personal attention. Particularly so, in the case of a red-bearded man, in a long linen duster, both heavily freighted with the red dust of the stage road, which seemed to have invaded his very eyes as he watched the landlord closely. Towards the close of the dinner, when Abner, accompanied by a negro waiter after his usual custom, passed down each side of the long table, collecting payment for the meal, the stranger looked up. "You air the landlord of this hotel, I reckon?"

"I am," said Abner tolerantly.

"I'd like a word or two with ye."

But Abner had been obliged to have a formula for such occasions. "Ye'll pay for yer dinner first," he said submissively, but firmly, "and make yer remarks agin the food arter."

The stranger flushed quickly, and his eye took an additional shade of red, but meeting Abner's serious gray ones, he contented himself with ostentatiously taking out a handful of gold and silver and paying his bill. Abner passed on, but after dinner was over he found the stranger in the hall.

"Ye pulled me up rather short in thar," said the man gloomily, "but it's just as well, as the talk I was wantin' with ye was kinder betwixt and between ourselves, and not hotel business. My name's Byers, and my wife let on she met ye down here."

For the first time it struck Abner as incongruous that another man should call Rosalie "his wife," although the fact of her remarriage had been made sufficiently plain to him. He accepted it as he would an earthquake, or any other dislocation, with his usual tolerant smile, and held out his hand.

Mr. Byers took it, seemingly mollified, and yet inwardly disturbed,—more even than was customary in Abner's guests after dinner.

"Have a drink with me," he suggested, although it had struck him that Mr. Byers had been drinking before dinner.

"I'm agreeable," responded Byers promptly; "but," with a glance at the crowded bar-room, "couldn't we go somewhere, jest you and me, and have a quiet confab?"

"I reckon. But ye must wait till we get her off."

Mr. Byers started slightly, but it appeared that the impedimental sex in this case was the coach, which, after a slight feminine hesitation, was at last started. Whereupon Mr. Langworthy, followed by a negro with a tray bearing a decanter and glasses, grasped Mr. Byers's arm, and walked along a small side veranda the depth of the house, stepped off, and apparently plunged with his guest into the primeval wilderness.

It has already been indicated that the site of the Big Flume Hotel had been scantily cleared; but Mr. Byers, backwoods-man though he was, was quite unprepared for so abrupt a change. The hotel, with its noisy crowd and garish newness, although scarcely a dozen yards away, seemed lost completely to sight and sound. A slight fringe of old tin cans, broken china, shavings, and even of the long-dried chips of the felled trees, once crossed, the two men were alone! From the tray, deposited at the foot of an enormous pine, they took the decanter, filled their glasses, and then disposed of themselves comfortably against a spreading root. The curling tail of a squirrel disappeared behind them; the far-off tap of a woodpecker accented the loneliness. And then, almost magically as it seemed, the thin veneering of civilization on the two men seemed to be cast off like the bark of the trees around them, and they lounged before each other in aboriginal freedom. Mr. Byers removed his restraining duster and undercoat. Mr. Langworthy resigned his dirty white jacket, his collar, and unloosed a suspender, with which he played.

"Would it be a fair question between two fa'r-minded men, ez hez lived alone," said Mr. Byers, with a gravity so supernatural that it could be referred only to liquor, "to ask ye in what sort o' way did Mrs. Byers show her temper?"

"Show her temper?" echoed Abner vacantly.

"Yes—in course, I mean when you and Mrs. Byers was—was—one? You know the di-vorce was for in-com-pat-ibility of temper."

"But she got the divorce from me, so I reckon I had the temper," said Langworthy, with great simplicity.

"Wha-at?" said Mr. Byers, putting down his glass and gazing with drunken gravity at the sad-eyed yet good-humoredly tolerant man before him. "You?—you had the temper?"

"I reckon that's what the court allowed," said Abner simply.

Mr. Byers stared. Then after a moment's pause he nodded with a significant yet relieved face. "Yes, I see, in course. Times when you'd h'isted too much o' this corn juice," lifting up his glass, "inside ye—ye sorter bu'st out ravin'?"

But Abner shook his head. "I wuz a total abstainer in them days," he said quietly.

Mr. Byers got unsteadily on his legs and looked around him. "Wot might hev bin the general gait o' your temper, pardner?" he said in a hoarse whisper.

"Don't know. I reckon that's jest whar the incompatibility kem in."

"And when she hove plates at your head, wot did you do?"

"She didn't hove no plates," said Abner gravely; "did she say she did?"

"No, no!" returned Byers hastily, in crimson confusion. "I kinder got it mixed with suthin' else." He waved his hand in a lordly way, as if dismissing the subject. "Howsumever, you and her is 'off' anyway," he added with badly concealed anxiety.

"I reckon: there's the decree," returned Abner, with his usual resigned acceptance of the fact.

"Mrs. Byers wuz allowin' ye wuz thinkin' of a second. How's that comin' on?"

"Jest whar it was," returned Abner. "I ain't doin' anything yet. Ye see I've got to tell the gal, naterally, that I'm di-vorced. And as that isn't known hereabouts, I don't keer to do so till I'm pretty certain. And then, in course, I've got to."

"Why hev ye 'got to'?" asked Byers abruptly.

"Because it wouldn't be on the square with the girl," said Abner. "How would you like it if Mrs. Byers had never told you she'd been married to me? And s'pose you'd happen to hev bin a di-vorced man and hadn't told her, eh? Well," he continued, sinking back resignedly against the tree, "I ain't sayin' anythin' but she'd hev got another di-vorce, and FROM you on the spot—you bet!"

"Well! all I kin say is," said Mr. Byers, lifting his voice

Bret Harte

excitedly, "that"—but he stopped short, and was about to fill his glass again from the decanter when the hand of Abner stopped him.

"Ye've got ez much ez ye kin carry now, Byers," he said slowly, "and that's about ez much ez I allow a man to take in at the Big Flume Hotel. Treatin' is treatin', hospitality is hospitality; ef you and me was squattin' out on the prairie I'd let you fill your skin with that pizen and wrap ye up in yer blankets afterwards. But here at Big Flume, the Stage Kempenny and the wimen and children passengers hez their rights." He paused a moment, and added, "And so I reckon hez Mrs. Byers, and I ain't goin' to send you home to her outer my house blind drunk. It's mighty rough on you and me, I know, but there's a lot o' roughness in this world ez hez to be got over, and life, ez far ez I kin see, ain't all a clearin'."

Perhaps it was his good-humored yet firm determination, perhaps it was his resigned philosophy, but something in the speaker's manner affected Mr. Byers's alcoholic suscepti- bility, and hastened his descent from the passionate heights of intoxication to the maudlin stage whither he was drifting. The fire of his red eyes became filmed and dim, an equal moisture gathered in his throat as he pressed Abner's hand with drunken fervor. "Thash so! your thinking o' me an' Mish Byersh is like troo fr'en'," he said thickly. "I wosh only goin' to shay that wotever Mish Byersh wosh—even if she wosh wife o' yours—she wosh—noble woman! Such a woman," continued Mr. Byers, dreamily regarding space, "can't have too many husbands."

"You jest sit back here a minit, and have a quiet smoke till I come back," said Abner, handing him his tobacco plug. "I've got to give the butcher his order—but I won't be a minit." He secured the decanter as he spoke, and evading an apparent disposition of his companion to fall upon his neck, made his way with long strides to the hotel, as Mr. Byers, sinking back against the trees, began certain futile efforts to light his unfilled pipe.

Whether Abner's attendance on the butcher was merely an excuse to withdraw with the decanter, I cannot say. He, however, dispatched his business quickly, and returned to the tree. But to his surprise Mr. Byers was no longer there. He explored the adjacent woodland with non-success, and no reply to his shouting. Annoyed but not alarmed, as it seemed probable that the missing man had fallen in a drunken sleep in some hidden shadows, he returned to the house, when it occurred to him that Byers might have sought the bar-room for some liquor. But he was still more surprised when the barkeeper volunteered the information that he had seen Mr. Byers hurriedly pass down the side veranda into the highroad. An hour later this was corroborated by an arriving teamster, who had passed a man answering to the description of Byers, "mor' 'n half full," staggeringly but hurriedly walking along the road "two miles back." There seemed to be no doubt that the missing man had taken himself off in a fit of indignation or of extreme thirst. Either hypothesis was disagreeable to Abner, in his queer sense of responsibility to Mrs. Byers, but he accepted it with his usual good-humored resignation.

Yet it was difficult to conceive what connection this episode had in his mind with his suspended attention to Mary Ellen, or why it should determine his purpose. But he had a logic of his own, and it seemed to have demonstrated to him that he must propose to the girl at once. This was no easy matter, however; he had never shown her any previous attention, and her particular functions in the hotel,—the charge of the few bedrooms for transient guests—seldom brought him in contact with her. His interview would have to appear to be a business one—which, however, he wished to avoid from a delicate consciousness of its truth. While making up his mind, for a few days he contented himself with gravely regarding her in his usual resigned, tolerant way, whenever he passed her. Unfortunately the first effect of this was an audible giggle from Mary Ellen, later some confusion and anxiety in her manner, and finally a demeanor of resentment and defiance.

This was so different from what he had expected that he was obliged to precipitate matters. The next day was Sunday,—a day on which his employees, in turns, were allowed the recreation of being driven to Big Flume City, eight miles distant, to church, or for the day's holiday. In the morning Mary Ellen was astonished by Abner informing her that he designed giving her a separate holiday with himself. It must be admitted that the girl, who was already "prinked up" for the enthrallment of the youth of Big Flume City, did not appear as delighted with the change of plan as a more exacting lover would have liked. Howbeit, as soon as the wagon had left with its occupants, Abner, in the unwonted disguise of a full suit of black clothes, turned to the girl, and offering her his arm, gravely proceeded along the side veranda across the mound of debris already described, to the adjacent wilderness and the very trees under which he and Byers had sat.

"It's about ez good a place for a little talk, Miss Budd," he said, pointing to a tree root, "ez ef we went a spell further, and it's handy to the house. And ef you'll jest say what you'd like outer the cupboard or the bar—no matter which—I'll fetch it to you."

But Mary Ellen Budd seated herself sideways on the root, with her furled white parasol in her lap, her skirts fastidiously tucked about her feet, and glancing at the fatuous Abner from under her stack of fluffy hair and light eyelashes, simply shook her head and said that "she reckoned she wasn't hankering much for anything" that morning.

"I've been calkilatin' to myself, Miss Budd," said Abner resignedly, "that when two folks—like ez you and me—meet together to kinder discuss things that might go so far ez to keep them together, if they hez had anything of that sort in their lives afore, they ought to speak of it confidentially like together."

"Ef any one o' them sneakin', soulless critters in the kitchen hez bin slingin' lies to ye about me—or carryin' tales," broke in Mary Ellen Budd, setting every one of her thirty-two strong, white teeth together with a snap, "well—ye might hev told me so to oncet without spilin' my Sunday! But ez fer yer keepin' me a minit longer, ye've only got to pay me my salary to-day and"—but here she stopped, for the astonishment in Abner's face was too plain to be misunderstood.

"Nobody's been slinging any lies about ye, Miss Budd," he said slowly, recovering himself resignedly from this last back-handed stroke of fate; "I warn't talkin' o' you, but myself. I was only allowin' to say that I was a di-vorced man."

As a sudden flush came over Mary Ellen's brownish-white face while she stared at him, Abner hastened to delicately explain. "It wasn't no onfaithfulness, Miss Budd—no philanderin' o' mine, but only 'incompatibility o' temper.'"

"Temper—your temper!" gasped Mary Ellen.

"Yes," said Abner.

And here a sudden change came over Mary Ellen's face, and she burst into a shriek of laughter. She laughed with her

Bret Harte

hands slapping the sides of her skirt, she laughed with her hands clasping her narrow, hollow waist, laughed with her head down on her knees and her fluffy hair tumbling over it. Abner was relieved, and yet it seemed strange to him that this revelation of his temper should provoke such manifest incredulity in both Byers and Mary Ellen. But perhaps these things would be made plain to him hereafter; at present they must be accepted "in the day's work" and tolerated.

"Your temper," gurgled Mary Ellen. "Saints alive! What kind o' temper?"

"Well, I reckon," returned Abner submissively, and selecting a word to give his meaning more comprehension,—"I reckon it was kinder—aggeravokin'."

Mary Ellen sniffed the air for a moment in speechless incredulity, and then, locking her hands around her knees and bending forward, said, "Look here! Ef that old woman o' yours ever knew what temper was in a man; ef she's ever bin tied to a brute that treated her like a nigger till she daren't say her soul was her own; who struck her with his eyes and tongue when he hadn't anythin' else handy; who made her life miserable when he was sober, and a terror when he was drunk; who at last drove her away, and then divorced her for desertion—then—then she might talk. But 'incompatibility o' temper' with you! Oh, go away—it makes me sick!"

How far Abner was impressed with the truth of this, how far it prompted his next question, nobody but Abner knew. For he said deliberately, "I was only goin' to ask ye, if, knowin' I was a di-vorced man, ye would mind marryin' me!"

Mary Ellen's face changed; the evasive instincts of her sex rose up. "Didn't I hear ye sayin' suthin' about refreshments," she said archly. "Mebbe you wouldn't mind gettin' me a bottle o' lemming sody outer the bar!"

Abner got up at once, perhaps not dismayed by this diversion, and departed for the refreshment. As he passed along the side veranda the recollection of Mr. Byers and his mysterious flight occurred to him. For a wild moment he thought of imitating him. But it was too late now—he had spoken. Besides, he had no wife to fly to, and the thirsty or indignant Byers had—his wife! Fate was indeed hard. He returned with the bottle of lemon soda on a tray and a resigned spirit equal to her decrees. Mary Ellen, remarking that he had brought nothing for himself, archly insisted upon his sharing with her the bottle of soda, and even coquettishly touched his lips with her glass. Abner smiled patiently.

But here, as if playfully exhilarated by the naughty foaming soda, she regarded him with her head—and a good deal of her blonde hair—very much on one side, as she said, "Do you know that all along o' you bein' so free with me in tellin' your affairs I kinder feel like just telling you mine?"

"Don't," said Abner promptly.

"Don't?" echoed Miss Budd.

"Don't," repeated Abner. "It's nothing to me. What I said about myself is different, for it might make some difference to you. But nothing you could say of yourself would make any change in me. I stick to what I said just now."

"But," said Miss Budd,—in half real, half simulated threatening,—"what if it had suthin' to do with my answer to what you said just now?"

"It couldn't. So, if it's all the same to you, Miss Budd, I'd rather ye wouldn't."

"That," said the lady still more archly, lifting a playful finger, "is your temper."

"Mebbe it is," said Abner suddenly, with a wondering sense of relief.

It was, however, settled that Miss Budd should go to Sacramento to visit her friends, that Abner would join her later, when their engagement would be announced, and that she should not return to the hotel until they were married. The compact was sealed by the interchange of a friendly kiss from Miss Budd with a patient, tolerating one from Abner, and then it suddenly occurred to them both that they might as well return to their duties in the hotel, which they did. Miss Budd's entire outing that Sunday lasted only half an hour.

A week elapsed. Miss Budd was in Sacramento, and the landlord of the Big Flume Hotel was standing at his usual post in the doorway during dinner, when a waiter handed him a note. It contained a single line scrawled in pencil:—

"Come out and see me behind the house as before. I dussent come in on account of her. C. BYERS."

"On account of 'her'!" Abner cast a hurried glance around the tables. Certainly Mrs. Byers was not there! He walked in the hall and the veranda—she was not there. He hastened to the rendezvous evidently meant by the writer, the wilderness behind the house. Sure enough, Byers, drunk and maudlin, supporting himself by the tree root, staggered forward, clasped him in his arms, and murmured hoarsely,—

"She's gone!"

"Gone?" echoed Abner, with a whitening face. "Mrs. Byers? Where?"

"Run away! Never come back no more! Gone!"

A vague idea that had been in Abner's mind since Byers's last visit now took awful shape. Before the unfortunate Byers could collect his senses he felt himself seized in a giant's grasp and forced against the tree.

"You coward!" said all that was left of the tolerant Abner— his even voice—"you hound! Did you dare to abuse her? to lay your vile hands on her—to strike her? Answer me."

The shock—the grasp—perhaps Abner's words, momentarily silenced Byers. "Did I strike her?" he said dazedly; "did I abuse her? Oh, yes!" with deep irony. "Certainly! In course! Look yer, pardner!"—he suddenly dragged up his sleeve from his red, hairy arm, exposing a blue cicatrix in its centre—"that's a jab from her scissors about three months ago; look yer!"—he bent his head and showed a scar along the scalp—"that's her playfulness with a fire shovel! Look yer!"—he quickly opened his collar, where his neck and cheek were striped and crossed with adhesive plaster— "that's all that was left o' a glass jar o' preserves—the preserves got away, but some of the glass got stuck! That's when she heard I was a di-vorced man and hadn't told her."

"Were you a di-vorced man?" gasped Abner.

"You know that; in course I was," said Byers scornfully; "d'ye meanter say she didn't tell ye?"

"She?" echoed Abner vaguely. "Your wife—you said just now she didn't know it before."

"My wife ez oncet was, I mean! Mary Ellen—your wife ez is to be," said Byers, with deep irony. "Oh, come now. Pretend ye don't know! Hi there! Hands off! Don't strike a man when he's down, like I am."

But Abner's clutch of Byers's shoulder relaxed, and he sank down to a sitting posture on the root. In the meantime Byers, overcome by a sense of this new misery added to his manifold grievances, gave way to maudlin silent tears.

"Mary Ellen—your first wife?" repeated Abner vacantly.

"Yesh!" said Byers thickly, "my first wife—shelected and picked out fer your shecond wife—by your first—like d—d conundrum. How wash I t'know?" he said, with a sudden shriek of public expostulation—"thash what I wanter know. Here I come to talk with fr'en', like man to man, unshuspecting, innoshent as chile, about my shecond wife! Fr'en' drops out, carryin' off the whiskey. Then I hear all o' suddent voice o' Mary Ellen talkin' in kitchen; then I come round softly and see Mary Ellen—my wife as useter be— standin' at fr'en's kitchen winder. Then I lights out quicker 'n lightnin' and scoots! And when I gets back home, I ups and tells my wife. And whosh fault ish't! Who shaid a man oughter tell hish wife? You! Who keepsh other mensh' first wivesh at kishen winder to frighten 'em to tell? You!"

But a change had already come over the face of Abner Langworthy. The anger, anxiety, astonishment, and vacuity that was there had vanished, and he looked up with his usual resigned acceptance of the inevitable as he said, "I reckon that's so! And seein' it's so," with good-natured tolerance, he added, "I reckon I'll break rules for oncet and stand ye another drink."

He stood another drink and yet another, and eventually put the doubly widowed Byers to bed in his own room. These were but details of a larger tribulation,—and yet he knew instinctively that his cup was not yet full. The further drop of bitterness came a few days later in a line from Mary Ellen: "I needn't tell you that all betwixt you and me is off, and you kin tell your old woman that her selection for a second wife for you wuz about as bad as your own first selection. Ye kin tell Mr. Byers—yer great friend whom ye never let on ye knew—that when I want another husband I shan't take the trouble to ask him to fish one out for me. It would be kind—but confusin'."

He never heard from her again. Mr. Byers was duly notified that Mrs. Byers had commenced action for divorce in another state in which concealment of a previous divorce invalidated the marriage, but he did not respond. The two men became great friends—and assured celibates. Yet they always spoke reverently of their "wife," with the touching prefix of "our."

"She was a good woman, pardner," said Byers.

"And she understood us," said Abner resignedly.

Perhaps she had.

A BUCKEYE HOLLOW INHERITANCE

The four men on the "Zip Coon" Ledge had not got fairly settled to their morning's work. There was the usual lingering hesitation which is apt to attend the taking-up of any regular or monotonous performance, shown in this instance in the prolonged scrutiny of a pick's point, the solemn selection of a shovel, or the "hefting" or weighing of a tapping-iron or drill. One member, becoming interested in a funny paragraph he found in the scrap of newspaper wrapped around his noonday cheese, shamelessly sat down to finish it, regardless of the prospecting pan thrown at him by another. They had taken up their daily routine of mining life like schoolboys at their tasks.

"Hello!" said Ned Wyngate, joyously recognizing a possible further interruption. "Blamed if the Express rider ain't comin' here!"

He was shading his eyes with his hand as he gazed over the broad sun-baked expanse of broken "flat" between them and the highroad. They all looked up, and saw the figure of a mounted man, with a courier's bag thrown over his shoulder, galloping towards them. It was really an event, as their letters were usually left at the grocery at the crossroads.

"I knew something was goin' to happen," said Wyngate. "I

didn't feel a bit like work this morning."

Here one of their number ran off to meet the advancing horseman. They watched him until they saw the latter rein up, and hand a brown envelope to their messenger, who ran breathlessly back with it to the Ledge as the horseman galloped away again.

"A telegraph for Jackson Wells," he said, handing it to the young man who had been reading the scrap of paper.

There was a dead silence. Telegrams were expensive rarities in those days, especially with the youthful Bohemian miners of the Zip Coon Ledge. They were burning with curiosity, yet a singular thing happened. Accustomed as they had been to a life of brotherly familiarity and unceremoniousness, this portentous message from the outside world of civilization recalled their old formal politeness. They looked steadily away from the receiver of the telegram, and he on his part stammered an apologetic "Excuse me, boys," as he broke the envelope.

There was another pause, which seemed to be interminable to the waiting partners. Then the voice of Wells, in quite natural tones, said, "By gum! that's funny! Read that, Dexter,—read it out loud."

Dexter Rice, the foreman, took the proffered telegram from Wells's hand, and read as follows:—

Your uncle, Quincy Wells, died yesterday, leaving you sole heir. Will attend you to-morrow for instructions.

BAKER AND TWIGGS,

Attorneys, Sacramento.

The three miners' faces lightened and turned joyously to Wells; but HIS face looked puzzled.

"May we congratulate you, Mr. Wells?" said Wyngate, with affected politeness; "or possibly your uncle may have been English, and a title goes with the 'prop,' and you may be Lord Wells, or Very Wells—at least."

But here Jackson Wells's youthful face lost its perplexity, and he began to laugh long and silently to himself. This was protracted to such an extent that Dexter asserted himself,—as foreman and senior partner.

"Look here, Jack! don't sit there cackling like a chuckle-headed magpie, if you ARE the heir."

"I—can't—help it," gasped Jackson. "I am the heir—but you see, boys, there AIN'T ANY PROPERTY."

"What do you mean? Is all that a sell?" demanded Rice.

"Not much! Telegraph's too expensive for that sort o' feelin'. You see, boys, I've got an Uncle Quincy, though I don't know him much, and he MAY be dead. But his whole fixin's consisted of a claim the size of ours, and played out long ago: a ramshackle lot o' sheds called a cottage, and a kind of market garden of about three acres, where he reared and sold vegetables. He was always poor, and as for calling it 'property,' and ME the 'heir'—good Lord!"

"A miser, as sure as you're born!" said Wyngate, with optimistic decision. "That's always the way. You'll find every crack of that blessed old shed stuck full of greenbacks and certificates of deposit, and lots of gold dust and coin buried all over that cow patch! And of course no one suspected it! And of course he lived alone, and never let any one get into his house—and nearly starved himself! Lord love you! There's hundreds of such cases. The world is full of 'em!"

"That's so," chimed in Pulaski Briggs, the fourth partner, "and I tell you what, Jacksey, we'll come over with you the day you take possession, and just 'prospect' the whole blamed shanty, pigsties, and potato patch, for fun—and won't charge you anything."

For a moment Jackson's face had really brightened under the infection of enthusiasm, but it presently settled into perplexity again.

"No! You bet the boys around Buckeye Hollow would have spotted anything like that long ago."

"Buckeye Hollow!" repeated Rice and his partners.

"Yes! Buckeye Hollow, that's the place; not twenty miles from here, and a God-forsaken hole, as you know."

A cloud had settled on Zip Coon Ledge. They knew of Buckeye Hollow, and it was evident that no good had ever yet come out of that Nazareth.

"There's no use of talking now," said Rice conclusively. "You'll draw it all from that lawyer shark who's coming here tomorrow, and you can bet your life he wouldn't have taken this trouble if there wasn't suthin' in it. Anyhow, we'll knock off work now and call it half a day, in honor of our distinguished young friend's accession to his baronial estates of Buckeye Hollow. We'll just toddle down to Tomlinson's at the cross-roads, and have a nip and a quiet game of old sledge at Jacksey's expense. I reckon the estate's good for THAT," he added, with severe gravity. "And, speaking as a fa'r-minded man and the president of this yer Company, if

Jackson would occasionally take out and air that telegraphic dispatch of his while we're at Tomlinson's, it might do something for that Company's credit—with Tomlinson! We're wantin' some new blastin' plant bad!"

Oddly enough the telegram—accidentally shown at Tomlinson's—produced a gratifying effect, and the Zip Coon Ledge materially advanced in public estimation. With this possible infusion of new capital into its resources, the Company was beset by offers of machinery and goods; and it was deemed expedient by the sapient Rice, that to prevent the dissemination of any more accurate information regarding Jackson's property the next day, the lawyer should be met at the stage office by one of the members, and conveyed secretly past Tomlinson's to the Ledge.

"I'd let you go," he said to Jackson, "only it won't do for that d—d skunk of a lawyer to think you're too anxious—sabe? We want to rub into him that we are in the habit out yer of havin' things left to us, and a fortin' more or less, falling into us now and then, ain't nothin' alongside of the Zip Coon claim. It won't hurt ye to keep up a big bluff on that hand of yours. Nobody would dare to 'call' you."

Indeed this idea was carried out with such elaboration the next day that Mr. Twiggs, the attorney, was considerably impressed both by the conduct of his guide, who (although burning with curiosity) expressed absolute indifference regarding Jackson Wells's inheritance, and the calmness of Jackson himself, who had to be ostentatiously called from his work on the Ledge to meet him, and who even gave him an audience in the hearing of his partners. Forced into an apologetic attitude, he expressed his regret at being obliged to bother Mr. Wells with an affair of such secondary importance, but he was obliged to carry out the formalities of the law.

"What do you suppose the estate is worth?" asked Wells carelessly.

"I should not think that the house, the claim, and the land would bring more than fifteen hundred dollars," replied Twiggs submissively.

To the impecunious owners of Zip Coon Ledge it seemed a large sum, but they did not show it.

"You see," continued Mr. Twiggs, "it's really a case of 'willing away' property from its obvious or direct inheritors, instead of a beneficial grant. I take it that you and your uncle were not particularly intimate,—at least, so I gathered when I made the will,—and his simple object was to disinherit his only daughter, with whom he had had some quarrel, and who had left him to live with his late wife's brother, Mr. Morley Brown, who is quite wealthy and residing in the same township. Perhaps you remember the young lady?"

Jackson Wells had a dim recollection of this cousin, a hateful, red-haired schoolgirl, and an equally unpleasant memory of this other uncle, who was purse-proud and had never taken any notice of him. He answered affirmatively.

"There may be some attempt to contest the will," continued Mr. Twiggs, "as the disinheriting of an only child and a daughter offends the sentiment of the people and of judges and jury, and the law makes such a will invalid, unless a reason is given. Fortunately your uncle has placed his reasons on record. I have a copy of the will here, and can show you the clause." He took it from his pocket, and read as follows: "'I exclude my daughter, Jocelinda Wells, from any benefit or provision of this my will and testament, for the reason that she has voluntarily abandoned her father's roof for the house of her mother's brother, Morley Brown; has preferred the fleshpots of Egypt to the virtuous frugalities of her own home, and has discarded the humble friends of her youth, and the associates of her father, for the meretricious and slavish sympathy of wealth and position. In lieu thereof, and as compensation therefor, I do hereby give and bequeath to her my full and free permission to gratify her frequently expressed wish for another guardian in place of myself, and to become the adopted daughter of the said Morley Brown, with the privilege of assuming the name of Brown as aforesaid.' You see," he continued, "as the young lady's present position is a better one than it would be if she were in her father's house, and was evidently a compromise, the sentimental consideration of her being left homeless and penniless falls to the ground. However, as the inheritance is small, and might be of little account to you, if you choose to waive it, I dare say we may make some arrangement."

This was an utterly unexpected idea to the Zip Coon Company, and Jackson Wells was for a moment silent. But Dexter Rice was equal to the emergency, and turned to the astonished lawyer with severe dignity.

"You'll excuse me for interferin', but, as the senior partner of this yer Ledge, and Jackson Wells yer bein' a most important member, what affects his usefulness on this claim affects us. And we propose to carry out this yer will, with all its dips and spurs and angles!"

As the surprised Twiggs turned from one to the other, Rice continued, "Ez far as we kin understand this little game, it's the just punishment of a high-flying girl as breaks her pore old father's heart, and the re-ward of a young feller ez has bin to our knowledge ez devoted a nephew as they make 'em. Time and time again, sittin' around our camp fire at night, we've heard Jacksey say,—kinder to himself, and kinder to us, 'Now I wonder what's gone o' old uncle Quincy;' and he never sat down to a square meal, or ever rose from a square game, but what he allus said, 'If old uncle Quince was only here now, boys, I'd die happy.' I leave it to you, gentlemen, if that wasn't Jackson Wells's gait all the time?"

There was a prolonged murmur of assent, and an affecting corroboration from Ned Wyngate of "That was him; that was Jacksey all the time!"

"Indeed, indeed," said the lawyer nervously. "I had quite the idea that there was very little fondness"—

"Not on your side—not on your side," said Rice quickly. "Uncle Quincy may not have anted up in this matter o' feelin', nor seen his nephew's rise. You know how it is yourself in these things—being a lawyer and a fa'r-minded man—it's all on one side, ginerally! There's always one who loves and sacrifices, and all that, and there's always one who rakes in the pot! That's the way o' the world; and that's why," continued Rice, abandoning his slightly philosophical attitude, and laying his hand tenderly, and yet with a singularly significant grip, on Wells's arm, "we say to him, 'Hang on to that will, and uncle Quincy's memory.' And we hev to say it. For he's that tender-hearted and keerless of money—having his own share in this Ledge—that ef that girl came whimperin' to him he'd let her take the 'prop' and let the hull thing slide! And then he'd remember that he had rewarded that gal that broke the old man's heart, and that would upset him again in his work. And there, you see, is just where WE come in! And we say, 'Hang on to that will like grim death!'"

The lawyer looked curiously at Rice and his companions, and then turned to Wells: "Nevertheless, I must look to you for instructions," he said dryly.

Bret Harte

But by this time Jackson Wells, although really dubious about supplanting the orphan, had gathered the sense of his partners, and said with a frank show of decision, "I think I must stand by the will."

"Then I'll have it proved," said Twiggs, rising. "In the meantime, if there is any talk of contesting"—

"If there is, you might say," suggested Wyngate, who felt he had not had a fair show in the little comedy,—"ye might say to that old skeesicks of a wife's brother, if he wants to nipple in, that there are four men on the Ledge—and four revolvers! We are gin'rally fa'r-minded, peaceful men, but when an old man's heart is broken, and his gray hairs brought down in sorrow to the grave, so to speak, we're bound to attend the funeral—sabe?"

When Mr. Twiggs had departed again, accompanied by a partner to guide him past the dangerous shoals of Tomlinson's grocery, Rice clapped his hand on Wells's shoulder. "If it hadn't been for me, sonny, that shark would have landed you into some compromise with that red-haired gal! I saw you weakenin', and then I chipped in. I may have piled up the agony a little on your love for old Quince, but if you aren't an ungrateful cub, that's how you ought to hev been feein', anyhow!"

Nevertheless, the youthful Wells, although touched by his elder partner's loyalty, and convinced of his own disinterestedness, felt a painful sense of lost chivalrous opportunity.

*****

On mature consideration it was finally settled that Jackson Wells should make his preliminary examination of his inheritance alone, as it might seem inconsistent with the previous indifferent attitude of his partners if they accompanied him. But he was implored to yield to no blandishments of the enemy, and to even make his visit a secret.

He went. The familiar flower-spiked trees which had given their name to Buckeye Hollow had never yielded entirely to improvements and the incursions of mining enterprise, and many of them had even survived the disused ditches, the scarred flats, the discarded levels, ruined flumes, and roofless cabins of the earlier occupation, so that when Jackson Wells entered the wide, straggling street of Buckeye, that summer morning was filled with the radiance of its blossoms and fragrant with their incense. His first visit there, ten years ago, had been a purely perfunctory and hasty one, yet he remembered the ostentatious hotel, built in the "flush time" of its prosperity, and already in a green premature decay; he recalled the Express Office and Town Hall, also passing away in a kind of similar green deliquescence; the little zinc church, now overgrown with fern and brambles, and the two or three fine substantial houses in the outskirts, which seemed to have sucked the vitality of the little settlement. One of these—he had been told—was the property of his rich and wicked maternal uncle, the hated appropriator of his red-headed cousin's affections. He recalled his brief visit to the departed testator's claim and market garden, and his by no means favorable impression of the lonely, crabbed old man, as well as his relief that his objectionable cousin, whom he had not seen since he was a boy, was then absent at the rival uncle's. He made his way across the road to a sunny slope where the market garden of three acres seemed to roll like a river of green rapids to a little "run" or brook, which, even in the dry season, showed a trickling rill. But here he was struck by a singular circumstance. The garden rested in a rich, alluvial soil, and under the quickening Californian sky had developed far beyond the ability of its late cultivator to restrain or keep it in order. Everything had grown luxuriantly, and in monstrous size and profusion. The garden had even trespassed its bounds, and impinged upon the open road, the deserted claims, and the ruins of the past. Stimulated by the little cultivation Quincy Wells had found time to give it, it had leaped its three acres and rioted through the Hollow. There were scarlet runners crossing the abandoned sluices, peas climbing the court-house wall, strawberries matting the trail, while the seeds and pollen of its few homely Eastern flowers had been blown far and wide through the woods. By a grim satire, Nature seemed to have been the only thing that still prospered in that settlement of man.

The cabin itself, built of unpainted boards, consisted of a sitting-room, dining-room, kitchen, and two bedrooms, all plainly furnished, although one of the bedrooms was better ordered, and displayed certain signs of feminine decoration, which made Jackson believe it had been his cousin's room. Luckily, the slight, temporary structure bore no deep traces of its previous occupancy to disturb him with its memories, and for the same reason it gained in cleanliness and freshness. The dry, desiccating summer wind that blew through it had carried away both the odors and the sense of domesticity; even the adobe hearth had no fireside tales to tell,—its very ashes had been scattered by the winds; and the gravestone of its dead owner on the hill was no more flavorless of his personality than was this plain house in which he had lived and died. The excessive vegetation produced by the stirred-up soil had covered and hidden the empty tin cans, broken boxes, and fragments of clothing which usually heaped and littered the tent-pegs of the pioneer. Nature's own profusion had thrust them into obscurity. Jackson Wells smiled as he recalled his sanguine partner's idea of a treasure-trove concealed and stuffed in the crevices of this tenement, already so palpably picked clean by those wholesome scavengers of California, the dry air and burning sun. Yet he was not displeased at this obliteration of a previous tenancy; there was the better chance for him to originate something. He whistled hopefully as he lounged, with his hands in his pockets, towards the only fence and gate that gave upon the road. Something stuck up on the gate-post attracted his attention. It was a sheet of paper bearing the inscription in a large hand: "Notice to trespassers. Look out for the Orphan Robber!" A plain signboard in faded black letters on the gate, which had borne the legend: "Quincy Wells, Dealer in Fruit and Vegetables," had been rudely altered in chalk to read: "Jackson Wells, Double Dealer in Wills and Codicils," and the intimation "Bouquets sold here" had been changed to "Bequests stole here." For an instant the simple-minded Jackson failed to discover any significance of this outrage, which seemed to him to be merely the wanton mischief of a schoolboy. But a sudden recollection of the lawyer's caution sent the blood to his cheeks and kindled his indignation. He tore down the paper and rubbed out the chalk interpolation—and then laughed at his own anger. Nevertheless, he would not have liked his belligerent partners to see it.

A little curious to know the extent of this feeling, he entered one of the shops, and by one or two questions which judiciously betrayed his ownership of the property, he elicited only a tradesman's interest in a possible future customer, and the ordinary curiosity about a stranger. The barkeeper of the hotel was civil, but brief and gloomy. He had heard the property was "willed away on account of some family quarrel which 'warn't none of his'." Mr. Wells would find Buckeye Hollow a mighty dull place after the mines. It was played out, sucked dry by two or three big mine owners who were trying to "freeze out" the other settlers, so as they might get the place to themselves and "boom it." Brown, who had the big house over the hill, was the head devil of the gang! Wells felt his indignation kindle anew. And this girl that he had ousted was Brown's friend. Was it possible that she was a party to Brown's designs to get this three acres with the other lands? If so, his long-suffering uncle was only just in his revenge.

He put all this diffidently before his partners on his return, and was a little startled at their adopting it with sanguine ferocity. They hoped that he would put an end to his thoughts of backing out of it. Such a course now would be dishonorable to his uncle's memory. It was clearly his duty to resist these blasted satraps of capitalists; he was providentially selected for the purpose—a village Hampden to withstand the tyrant. "And I reckon that shark of a lawyer knew all about it when he was gettin' off that 'purp stuff' about people's sympathies with the girl," said Rice belligerently. "Contest the will, would he? Why, if we caught that Brown with a finger in the pie we'd just whip up the boys on this Ledge and lynch him. You hang on to that three acres and the garden patch of your forefathers, sonny, and we'll see you through!"

Nevertheless, it was with some misgivings that Wells consented that his three partners should actually accompany him and see him put in peaceable possession of his inheritance. His instinct told him that there would be no contest of the will, and still less any opposition on the part of the objectionable relative, Brown. When the wagon which contained his personal effects and the few articles of furniture necessary for his occupancy of the cabin arrived, the exaggerated swagger which his companions had put on in their passage through the settlement gave way to a pastoral indolence, equally half real, half affected. Lying on their backs under a buckeye, they permitted Rice to voice the general sentiment. "There's a suthin' soothin' and dreamy in this kind o' life, Jacksey, and we'll make a point of comin' here for a couple of days every two weeks to lend you a hand; it will be a mighty good change from our nigger work on the claim."

In spite of this assurance, and the fact that they had voluntarily come to help him put the place in order, they did very little beyond lending a cheering expression of unqualified praise and unstinted advice. At the end of four hours' weeding and trimming the boundaries of the garden, they unanimously gave their opinion that it would be more systematic for him to employ Chinese labor at once.

"You see," said Ned Wyngate, "the Chinese naturally take to this kind o' business. Why, you can't take up a china plate or saucer but you see 'em pictured there working at jobs like this, and they kin live on green things and rice that cost nothin', and chickens. You'll keep chickens, of course."

Jackson thought that his hands would be full enough with the garden, but he meekly assented.

"I'll get a pair—you only want two to begin with," continued Wyngate cheerfully, "and in a month or two you've got all you want, and eggs enough for market. On second thoughts, I don't know whether you hadn't better begin with eggs first. That is, you borry some eggs from one man and a hen from another. Then you set 'em, and when the chickens are hatched out you just return the hen to the second man, and the eggs, when your chickens begin to lay, to the first man, and you've got your chickens for nothing—and there you are."

This ingenious proposition, which was delivered on the last slope of the domain, where the partners were lying exhausted from their work, was broken in upon by the appearance of a small boy, barefooted, sunburnt, and tow-headed, who, after a moment's hurried scrutiny of the group, threw a letter with unerring precision into the lap of Jackson Wells, and then fled precipitately. Jackson instinctively suspected he was connected with the outrage on his fence and gate-post, but as he had avoided telling his partners of the incident, fearing to increase their belligerent attitude, he felt now an awkward consciousness mingled with his indignation as he broke the seal and read as follows:—

SIR,—This is to inform you that although you have got hold of the property by underhanded and sneaking ways, you ain't no right to touch or lay your vile hands on the Cherokee Rose alongside the house, nor on the Giant of Battles, nor on the Maiden's Pride by the gate—the same being the property of Miss Jocelinda Wells, and planted by her, under the penalty of the Law. And if you, or any of your gang of ruffians, touches it or them, or any thereof, or don't deliver it up when called for in good order, you will be persecuted by them.

AVENGER.

It is to be feared that Jackson would have suppressed this also, but the keen eyes of his partners, excited by the abruptness of the messenger, were upon him. He smiled feebly, and laid the letter before them. But he was unprepared for their exaggerated indignation, and with difficulty restrained them from dashing off in the direction of the vanished herald. "And what could you do?" he said. "The boy's only a messenger."

"I'll get at that d—d skunk Brown, who's back of him," said Dexter Rice.

"And what then?" persisted Jackson, with a certain show of independence. "If this stuff belongs to the girl, I'm not certain I shan't give them up without any fuss. Lord! I want nothing but what the old man left me—and certainly nothing of HERS."

Here Ned Wyngate was heard to murmur that Jackson was one of those men who would lie down and let coyotes crawl over him if they first presented a girl's visiting card, but he was stopped by Rice demanding paper and pencil. The former being torn from a memorandum book, and a stub of the latter produced from another pocket, he wrote as follows:—

SIR,—In reply to the hogwash you have kindly exuded in your letter of to-day, I have to inform you that you can have what you ask for Miss Wells, and perhaps a trifle on your own account, by calling this afternoon on—Yours truly—

"Now, sign it," continued Rice, handing him the pencil.

"But this will look as if we were angry and wanted to keep the plants," protested Wells.

"Never you mind, sonny, but sign! Leave the rest to your partners, and when you lay your head on your pillow to-night return thanks to an overruling Providence for providing you with the right gang of ruffians to look after you!"

Wells signed reluctantly, and Wyngate offered to find a Chinaman in the gulch who would take the missive. "And being a Chinaman, Brown can do any cussin' or buck talk THROUGH him!" he added.

The afternoon wore on; the tall Douglas pines near the water pools wheeled their long shadows round and halfway up the slope, and the sun began to peer into the faces of the reclining men. Subtle odors of mint and southern-wood, stragglers from the garden, bruised by their limbs, replaced the fumes of their smoked-out pipes, and the hammers of the woodpeckers were busy in the grove as they lay lazily nibbling the fragrant leaves like peaceful ruminants. Then came the sound of approaching wheels along the invisible highway beyond the buckeyes, and then a halt and silence. Rice rose slowly, bright pin points in the pupils of his gray eyes.

"Bringin' a wagon with him to tote the hull shanty away," suggested Wyngate.

"Or fetched his own ambulance," said Briggs.

Nevertheless, after a pause, the wheels presently rolled away again.

"We'd better go and meet him at the gate," said Rice, hitching his revolver holster nearer his hip. "That wagon stopped long enough to put down three or four men."

They walked leisurely but silently to the gate. It is probable that none of them believed in a serious collision, but now the prospect had enough possibility in it to quicken their pulses. They reached the gate. But it was still closed; the road beyond it empty.

"Mebbe they've sneaked round to the cabin," said Briggs, "and are holdin' it inside."

They were turning quickly in that direction, when Wyngate said, "Hush!—some one's there in the brush under the buckeyes."

They listened; there was a faint rustling in the shadows.

"Come out o' that, Brown—into the open. Don't be shy,"

called out Rice in cheerful irony. "We're waitin' for ye."

But Briggs, who was nearest the wood, here suddenly uttered an exclamation,—"B'gosh!" and fell back, open-mouthed, upon his companions. They too, in another moment, broke into a feeble laugh, and lapsed against each other in sheepish silence. For a very pretty girl, handsomely dressed, swept out of the wood and advanced towards them.

Even at any time she would have been an enchanting vision to these men, but in the glow of exercise and sparkle of anger she was bewildering. Her wonderful hair, the color of freshly hewn redwood, had escaped from her hat in her passage through the underbrush, and even as she swept down upon them in her majesty she was jabbing a hairpin into it with a dexterous feminine hand.

The three partners turned quite the color of her hair; Jackson Wells alone remained white and rigid. She came on, her very short upper lip showing her white teeth with her panting breath.

Rice was first to speak. "I beg—your pardon, Miss—I thought it was Brown—you know," he stammered.

But she only turned a blighting brown eye on the culprit, curled her short lip till it almost vanished in her scornful nostrils, drew her skirt aside with a jerk, and continued her way straight to Jackson Wells, where she halted.

"We did not know you were—here alone," he said apologetically.

"Thought I was afraid to come alone, didn't you? Well, you see, I'm not. There!" She made another dive at her hat and hair, and brought the hat down wickedly over her eyebrows.

"Gimme my plants."

Jackson had been astonished. He would have scarcely recognized in this willful beauty the red-haired girl whom he had boyishly hated, and with whom he had often quarreled. But there was a recollection—and with that recollection came an instinct of habit. He looked her squarely in the face, and, to the horror of his partners, said, "Say please!"

They had expected to see him fall, smitten with the hairpin! But she only stopped, and then in bitter irony said, "Please, Mr. Jackson Wells."

"I haven't dug them up yet—and it would serve you just right if I made you get them for yourself. But perhaps my friends here might help you—if you were civil."

The three partners seized spades and hoes and rushed forward eagerly. "Only show us what you want," they said in one voice. The young girl stared at them, and at Jackson. Then with swift determination she turned her back scornfully upon him, and with a dazzling smile which reduced the three men to absolute idiocy, said to the others, "I'll show YOU," and marched away to the cabin.

"Ye mustn't mind Jacksey," said Rice, sycophantically edging to her side, "he's so cut up with losin' your father that he loved like a son, he isn't himself, and don't seem to know whether to ante up or pass out. And as for yourself, Miss—why—What was it he was sayin' only just as the young lady came?" he added, turning abruptly to Wyngate.

"Everything that cousin Josey planted with her own hands must be took up carefully and sent back—even though it's killin' me to part with it," quoted Wyngate unblushingly, as he slouched along on the other side.

Miss Wells's eyes glared at them, though her mouth still smiled ravishingly. "I'm sure I'm troubling you."

In a few moments the plants were dug up and carefully laid together; indeed, the servile Briggs had added a few that she had not indicated.

"Would you mind bringing them as far as the buggy that's coming down the hill?" she said, pointing to a buggy driven by a small boy which was slowly approaching the gate. The men tenderly lifted the uprooted plants, and proceeded solemnly, Miss Wells bringing up the rear, towards the gate, where Jackson Wells was still surlily lounging.

They passed out first. Miss Wells lingered for an instant, and then advancing her beautiful but audacious face within an inch of Jackson's, hissed out, "Make-believe! and hypocrite!"

"Cross-patch and sauce-box!" returned Jackson readily, still under the malign influence of his boyish past, as she flounced away.

Presently he heard the buggy rattle away with his persecutor. But his partners still lingered on the road in earnest conversation, and when they did return it was with a singular awkwardness and embarrassment, which he naturally put down to a guilty consciousness of their foolish weakness in succumbing to the girl's demands.

But he was a little surprised when Dexter Rice approached him gloomily. "Of course," he began, "it ain't no call of ours to interfere in family affairs, and you've a right to keep 'em to yourself, but if you'd been fair and square and above board in what you got off on us about this per—"

"What do you mean?" demanded the astonished Wells.

"Well—callin' her a 'red-haired gal.'"

"Well—she is a red-haired girl!" said Wells impatiently.

"A man," continued Rice pityingly, "that is so prejudiced as to apply such language to a beautiful orphan—torn with grief at the loss of a beloved but d—d misconstruing parent— merely because she begs a few vegetables out of his potato patch, ain't to be reasoned with. But when you come to look at this thing by and large, and as a fa'r-minded man, sonny, you'll agree with us that the sooner you make terms with her the better. Considerin' your interest, Jacksey,—let alone the claims of humanity,—we've concluded to withdraw from here until this thing is settled. She's sort o' mixed us up with your feelings agin her, and naturally supposed we object to the color of her hair! and bein' a penniless orphan, rejected by her relations"—

"What stuff are you talking?" burst in Jackson. "Why, YOU saw she treated you better than she did me."

"Steady! There you go with that temper of yours that frightened the girl! Of course she could see that WE were fa'r-minded men, accustomed to the ways of society, and not upset by the visit of a lady, or the givin' up of a few green sticks! But let that slide! We're goin' back home to-night, sonny, and when you've thought this thing over and are straightened up and get your right bearin's, we'll stand by you as before. We'll put a man on to do your work on the Ledge, so ye needn't worry about that."

They were quite firm in this decision,—however absurd or obscure their conclusions,—and Jackson, after his first flash of indignation, felt a certain relief in their departure. But strangely enough, while he had hesitated about keeping the property when they were violently in favor of it, he now felt he was right in retaining it against their advice to compromise. The sentimental idea had vanished with his recognition of his hateful cousin in the role of the injured orphan. And for the same odd reason her prettiness only increased his resentment. He was not deceived,—it was the same capricious, willful, red-haired girl.

The next day he set himself to work with that dogged steadiness that belonged to his simple nature, and which had endeared him to his partners. He set half a dozen Chinamen to work, and followed, although apparently directing, their methods. The great difficulty was to restrain and control the excessive vegetation, and he matched the small economies of the Chinese against the opulence of the Californian soil. The "garden patch" prospered; the neighbors spoke well of it and of him. But Jackson knew that this fierce harvest of early spring was to be followed by the sterility of the dry season, and that irrigation could alone make his work profitable in the end. He brought a pump to force the water from the little stream at the foot of the slope to the top, and allowed it to flow back through parallel trenches. Again Buckeye applauded! Only the gloomy barkeeper shook his head. "The moment you get that thing to pay, Mr. Wells, you'll find the hand of Brown, somewhere, getting ready to squeeze it dry!"

But Jackson Wells did not trouble himself about Brown, whom he scarcely knew. Once indeed, while trenching the slope, he was conscious that he was watched by two men from the opposite bank; but they were apparently satisfied by their scrutiny, and turned away. Still less did he concern himself with the movements of his cousin, who once or twice passed him superciliously in her buggy on the road. Again, she met him as one of a cavalcade of riders, mounted on a handsome but ill-tempered mustang, which she was managing with an ill-temper and grace equal to the brute's, to the alternate delight and terror of her cavalier. He could see that she had been petted and spoiled by her new guardian and his friends far beyond his conception. But why she should grudge him the little garden and the pastoral life for which she was so unsuited, puzzled him greatly.

One afternoon he was working near the road, when he was startled by an outcry from his Chinese laborers, their rapid dispersal from the strawberry beds where they were working, the splintering crash of his fence rails, and a commotion among the buckeyes. Furious at what seemed to him one of the usual wanton attacks upon coolie labor, he seized his pick and ran to their assistance. But he was surprised to find Jocelinda's mustang caught by the saddle and struggling between two trees, and its unfortunate mistress lying upon the strawberry bed. Shocked but cool-headed, Jackson released the horse first, who was lashing out and destroying everything within his reach, and then turned to his cousin. But she had already lifted herself to her elbow, and with a trickle of blood and mud on one fair cheek was surveying him scornfully under her tumbled hair and hanging hat.

"You don't suppose I was trespassing on your wretched patch again, do you?" she said in a voice she was trying to keep from breaking. "It was that brute—who bolted."

"I don't suppose you were bullying ME this time," he said, "but you were YOUR HORSE—or it wouldn't have happened. Are you hurt?"

She tried to move; he offered her his hand, but she shied from it and struggled to her feet. She took a step forward—but limped.

"If you don't want my arm, let me call a Chinaman," he suggested.

She glared at him. "If you do I'll scream!" she said in a low voice, and he knew she would. But at the same moment her face whitened, at which he slipped his arm under hers in a dexterous, business-like way, so as to support her weight. Then her hat got askew, and down came a long braid over his shoulder. He remembered it of old, only it was darker than then and two or three feet longer.

"If you could manage to limp as far as the gate and sit down on the bank, I'd get your horse for you," he said. "I hitched it to a sapling."

"I saw you did—before you even offered to help me," she said scornfully.

"The horse would have got away—YOU couldn't."

"If you only knew how I hated you," she said, with a white face, but a trembling lip.

"I don't see how that would make things any better," he said. "Better wipe your face; it's scratched and muddy, and you've been rubbing your nose in my strawberry bed."

She snatched his proffered handkerchief suddenly, applied it to her face, and said: "I suppose it looks dreadful."

"Like a pig's," he returned cheerfully.

She walked a little more firmly after this, until they reached the gate. He seated her on the bank, and went back for the mustang. That beautiful brute, astounded and sore from its contact with the top rail and brambles, was cowed and subdued as he led it back.

She had finished wiping her face, and was hurriedly

disentangling two stinging tears from her long lashes, before she threw back his handkerchief. Her sprained ankle obliged him to lift her into the saddle and adjust her little shoe in the stirrup. He remembered when it was still smaller. "You used to ride astride," he said, a flood of recollection coming over him, "and it's much safer with your temper and that brute."

"And you," she said in a lower voice, "used to be"—But the rest of her sentence was lost in the switch of the whip and the jump of her horse, but he thought the word was "kinder."

Perhaps this was why, after he watched her canter away, he went back to the garden, and from the bruised and trampled strawberry bed gathered a small basket of the finest fruit, covered them with leaves, added a paper with the highly ingenious witticism, "Picked up with you," and sent them to her by one of the Chinamen. Her forcible entry moved Li Sing, his foreman, also chief laundryman to the settlement, to reminiscences:

"Me heap knew Missy Wells and ole man, who go dead. Ole man allee time make chin music to Missy. Allee time jaw jaw—allee time make lows—allee time cuttee up Missy! Plenty time lockee up Missy topside house; no can walkee—no can talkee—no hab got—how can get?—must washee washee allee same Chinaman. Ole man go dead—Missy all lightee now. Plenty fun. Plenty stay in Blown's big house, top-side hill; Blown first-chop man."

Had he inquired he might have found this pagan testimony, for once, corroborated by the Christian neighbors.

But another incident drove all this from his mind. The little stream—the life blood of his garden—ran dry! Inquiry showed that it had been diverted two miles away into Brown's ditch! Wells's indignant protest elicited a formal reply from Brown, stating that he owned the adjacent mining claims, and reminding him that mining rights to water took precedence of the agricultural claim, but offering, by way of compensation, to purchase the land thus made useless and sterile. Jackson suddenly recalled the prophecy of the gloomy barkeeper. The end, had come! But what could the scheming capitalist want with the land, equally useless—as his uncle had proved—for mining purposes? Could it be sheer malignity, incited by his vengeful cousin? But here he paused, rejecting the idea as quickly as it came. No! his partners were right! He was a trespasser on his cousin's heritage—there was no luck in it—he was wrong, and this was his punishment! Instead of yielding gracefully as he might, he must back down now, and she would never know his first real feelings. Even now he would make over the property to her as a free gift. But his partners had advanced him money from their scanty means to plant and work it. He believed that an appeal to their feelings would persuade them to forego even that, but he shrank even more from confessing his defeat to THEM than to her.

He had little heart in his labors that day, and dismissed the Chinamen early. He again examined his uncle's old mining claim on the top of the slope, but was satisfied that it had been a hopeless enterprise and wisely abandoned. It was sunset when he stood under the buckeyes, gloomily looking at the glow fade out of the west, as it had out of his boyish hopes. He had grown to like the place. It was the hour, too, when the few flowers he had cultivated gave back their pleasant odors, as if grateful for his care. And then he heard his name called.

It was his cousin, standing a few yards from him in evident hesitation. She was quite pale, and for a moment he thought she was still suffering from her fall, until he saw in her nervous, half-embarrassed manner that it had no physical cause. Her old audacity and anger seemed gone, yet there was a queer determination in her pretty brows.

"Good-evening," he said.

She did not return his greeting, but pulling uneasily at her glove, said hesitatingly: "Uncle has asked you to sell him this land?"

"Yes."

"Well—don't!" she burst out abruptly.

He stared at her.

"Oh, I'm not trying to keep you here," she went on, flashing back into her old temper; "so you needn't stare like that. I say, 'Don't,' because it ain't right, it ain't fair."

"Why, he's left me no alternative," he said.

"That's just it—that's why it's mean and low. I don't care if he is our uncle."

Jackson was bewildered and shocked.

"I know it's horrid to say it," she said, with a white face; "but it's horrider to keep it in! Oh, Jack! when we were little, and used to fight and quarrel, I never was mean—was I? I never was underhanded—was I? I never lied—did I? And I can't lie now. Jack," she looked hurriedly around her, "HE wants to get hold of the land—HE thinks there's gold in the slope and bank by the stream. He says dad was a fool to have located his claim so high up. Jack! did you ever prospect the bank?"

A dawning of intelligence came upon Jackson. "No," he said;

"but," he added bitterly, "what's the use? He owns the water now,—I couldn't work it."

"But, Jack, IF you found the color, this would be a MINING claim! You could claim the water right; and, as it's your land, your claim would be first!"

Jackson was startled. "Yes, IF I found the color."

"You WOULD find it."

"WOULD?"

"Yes! I DID—on the sly! Yesterday morning on your slope by the stream, when no one was up! I washed a panful and got that." She took a piece of tissue paper from her pocket, opened it, and shook into her little palm three tiny pin points of gold.

"And that was your own idea, Jossy?"

"Yes!"

"Your very own?"

"Honest Injin!"

"Wish you may die?"

"True, O King!"

He opened his arms, and they mutually embraced. Then they separated, taking hold of each other's hands solemnly, and falling back until they were at arm's length. Then they slowly extended their arms sideways at full length, until this action naturally brought their faces and lips together. They did this with the utmost gravity three times, and then embraced again, rocking on pivoted feet like a metronome. Alas! it was no momentary inspiration. The most casual and indifferent observer could see that it was the result of long previous practice and shameless experience. And as such—it was a revelation and an explanation.

*****

"I always suspected that Jackson was playin' us about that red-haired cousin," said Rice two weeks later; "but I can't swallow that purp stuff about her puttin' him up to that dodge about a new gold discovery on a fresh claim, just to knock out Brown. No, sir. He found that gold in openin' these irrigatin' trenches,—the usual nigger luck, findin' what you're not lookin' arter."

"Well, we can't complain, for he's offered to work it on shares with us," said Briggs.

"Yes—until he's ready to take in another partner."

"Not—Brown?" said his horrified companions.

"No!—but Brown's adopted daughter—that red-haired cousin!"

THE REINCARNATION OF SMITH

The extravagant supper party by which Mr. James Farendell celebrated the last day of his bachelorhood was protracted so far into the night, that the last guest who parted from him at the door of the principal Sacramento restaurant was for a moment impressed with the belief that a certain ruddy glow in the sky was already the dawn. But Mr. Farendell had kept his head clear enough to recognize it as the light of some burning building in a remote business district, a not infrequent occurrence in the dry season. When he had dismissed his guest he turned away in that direction for further information. His own counting-house was not in that immediate neighborhood, but Sacramento had been once before visited by a rapid and far-sweeping conflagration, and it behooved him to be on the alert even on this night of festivity.

Perhaps also a certain anxiety arose out of the occasion. He was to be married to-morrow to the widow of his late partner, and the marriage, besides being an attractive one, would settle many business difficulties. He had been a fortunate man, but, like many more fortunate men, was not blind to the possibilities of a change of luck. The death of his partner in a successful business had at first seemed to betoken that change, but his successful, though hasty, courtship of the inexperienced widow had restored his chances without greatly shocking the decorum of a pioneer

Bret Harte

community. Nevertheless, he was not a contented man, and hardly a determined—although an energetic one.

A walk of a few moments brought him to the levee of the river,—a favored district, where his counting-house, with many others, was conveniently situated. In these early days only a few of these buildings could be said to be permanent,—fire and flood perpetually threatened them. They were merely temporary structures of wood, or in the case of Mr. Farendell's office, a shell of corrugated iron, sheathing a one-storied wooden frame, more or less elaborate in its interior decorations. By the time he had reached it, the distant fire had increased. On his way he had met and recognized many of his business acquaintances hurrying thither,—some to save their own property, or to assist the imperfectly equipped volunteer fire department in their unselfish labors. It was probably Mr. Farendell's peculiar preoccupation on that particular night which had prevented his joining in their brotherly zeal.

He unlocked the iron door, and lit the hanging lamp that was used in all-night sittings on steamer days. It revealed a smartly furnished office, with a high desk for his clerks, and a smaller one for himself in one corner. In the centre of the wall stood a large safe. This he also unlocked and took out a few important books, as well as a small drawer containing gold coin and dust to the amount of about five hundred dollars, the large balance having been deposited in bank on the previous day. The act was only precautionary, as he did not exhibit any haste in removing them to a place of safety, and remained meditatively absorbed in looking over a packet of papers taken from the same drawer. The closely shuttered building, almost hermetically sealed against light, and perhaps sound, prevented his observing the steadily increasing light of the conflagration, or hearing the nearer tumult of the firemen, and the invasion of his quiet district by other equally solicitous tenants. The papers seemed also to possess some importance, for, the stillness being suddenly broken by the turning of the handle of the heavy door he had just closed, and its opening with difficulty, his first act was to hurriedly conceal them, without apparently paying a thought to the exposed gold before him. And his expression and attitude in facing round towards the door was quite as much of nervous secretiveness as of indignation at the interruption.

Yet the intruder appeared, though singular, by no means formidable. He was a man slightly past the middle age, with a thin face, hollowed at the cheeks and temples as if by illness or asceticism, and a grayish beard that encircled his throat like a soiled worsted "comforter" below his clean-shaven chin and mouth. His manner was slow and methodical, and even when he shot the bolt of the door behind him, the act did not seem aggressive. Nevertheless Mr. Farendell half rose with his hand on his pistol-pocket, but the stranger merely lifted his own hand with a gesture of indifferent warning, and, drawing a chair towards him, dropped into it deliberately.

Mr. Farendell's angry stare changed suddenly to one of surprised recognition. "Josh Scranton," he said hesitatingly.

"I reckon," responded the stranger slowly. "That's the name I allus bore, and YOU called yourself Farendell. Well, we ain't seen each other sens the spring o' '50, when ye left me lying nigh petered out with chills and fever on the Stanislaus River, and sold the claim that me and Duffy worked under our very feet, and skedaddled for 'Frisco!"

"I only exercised my right as principal owner, and to secure my advances," began the late Mr. Farendell sharply.

But again the thin hand was raised, this time with a slow, scornful waiving of any explanations. "It ain't that in partickler that I've kem to see ye for to-night," said the stranger slowly, "nor it ain't about your takin' the name o' 'Farendell,' that friend o' yours who died on the passage here with ye, and whose papers ye borrowed! Nor it ain't on account o' that wife of yours ye left behind in Missouri, and whose letters you never answered. It's them things all together—and suthin' else!"

"What the d—l do you want, then?" said Farendell, with a desperate directness that was, however, a tacit confession of the truth of these accusations.

"Yer allowin' that ye'll get married tomorrow?" said Scranton slowly.

"Yes, and be d—d to you," said Farendell fiercely.

"Yer NOT," returned Scranton. "Not if I knows it. Yer goin' to climb down. Yer goin' to get up and get! Yer goin' to step down and out! Yer goin' to shut up your desk and your books and this hull consarn inside of an hour, and vamose the ranch. Arter an hour from now thar won't be any Mr. Farendell, and no weddin' to-morrow."

"If that's your game—perhaps you'd like to murder me at once?" said Farendell with a shifting eye, as his hand again moved towards his revolver.

But again the thin hand of the stranger was also lifted. "We ain't in the business o' murderin' or bein' murdered, or we might hev kem here together, me and Duffy. Now if anything happens to me Duffy will be left, and HE'S got the proofs."

Farendell seemed to recognize the fact with the same directness. "That's it, is it?" he said bluntly. "Well, how much do you want? Only, I warn you that I haven't much to give."

"Wotever you've got, if it was millions, it ain't enough to buy us up, and ye ought to know that by this time," responded Scranton, with a momentary flash in his eyes. But the next moment his previous passionless deliberation returned, and leaning his arm on the desk of the man before him he picked up a paperweight carelessly and turned it over as he said slowly, "The fact is, Mr. Farendell, you've been making us, me and Duffy, tired. We've bin watchin' you and your doin's, lyin' low and sayin' nothin', till we concluded that it was about time you handed in your checks and left the board. We ain't wanted nothin' of ye, we ain't begrudged ye nothin', but we've allowed that this yer thing must stop."

"And what if I refuse?" said Farendell.

"Thar'll be some cussin' and a big row from YOU, I kalkilate—and maybe some fightin' all round," said Scranton dispassionately. "But it will be all the same in the end. The hull thing will come out, and you'll hev to slide just the same. T'otherwise, ef ye slide out NOW, it's without a row."

"And do you suppose a business man like me can disappear without a fuss over it?" said Farendell angrily. "Are you mad?"

"I reckon the hole YOU'LL make kin be filled up," said Scranton dryly. "But ef ye go NOW, you won't be bothered by the fuss, while if you stay you'll have to face the music, and go too!"

Farendell was silent. Possibly the truth of this had long since been borne upon him. No one but himself knew the incessant strain of these years of evasion and concealment, and how he often had been near to some such desperate culmination. The sacrifice offered to him was not, therefore, so great as it might have seemed. The knowledge of this might have given him a momentary superiority over his antagonist had Scranton's motive been a purely selfish or malignant one, but as it was not, and as he may have had some instinctive idea of Farendell's feeling also, it made his ultimatum appear the more passionless and fateful. And it was this quality which perhaps caused Farendell to burst out with desperate abruptness,—

"What in h-ll ever put you up to this!"

Scranton folded his arms upon Farendell's desk, and slowly wiping his clean jaw with one hand, repeated deliberately, "Wall—I reckon I told ye that before! You've been making us—me and Duffy—tired!" He paused for a moment, and then, rising abruptly, with a careless gesture towards the uncovered tray of gold, said, "Come! ye kin take enuff o' that to get away with; the less ye take, though, the less likely you'll be to be followed!"

He went to the door, unlocked and opened it. A strange light, as of a lurid storm interspersed by sheet-like lightning, filled the outer darkness, and the silence was now broken by dull crashes and nearer cries and shouting. A few figures were also dimly flitting around the neighboring empty offices, some of which, like Farendell's, had been entered by their now alarmed owners.

"You've got a good chance now," continued Scranton; "ye couldn't hev a better. It's a big fire—a scorcher—and jest the time for a man to wipe himself out and not be missed. Make tracks where the crowd is thickest and whar ye're likely to be seen, ez ef ye were helpin'! Ther' 'll be other men missed tomorrow beside you," he added with grim significance; "but nobody'll know that you was one who really got away."

Where the imperturbable logic of the strange man might have failed, the noise, the tumult, the suggestion of swift-coming disaster, and the necessity for some immediate action of any kind, was convincing. Farendell hastily stuffed his pockets with gold and the papers he had found, and moved to the door. Already he fancied he felt the hot breath of the leaping conflagration beyond. "And you?" he said, turning suspiciously to Scranton.

"When you're shut of this and clean off, I'll fix things and leave too—but not before. I reckon," he added grimly, with a glance at the sky, now streaming with sparks like a meteoric shower, "thar won't be much left here in the morning."

A few dull embers pattered on the iron roof of the low building and bounded off in ashes. Farendell cast a final glance around him, and then darted from the building. The iron door clanged behind him—he was gone.

Evidently not too soon, for the other buildings were already deserted by their would-be salvors, who had filled the streets with piles of books and valuables waiting to be carried away. Then occurred a terrible phenomenon, which had once before in such disasters paralyzed the efforts of the firemen. A large wooden warehouse in the centre of the block of offices, many hundred feet from the scene of active conflagration—which had hitherto remained intact—suddenly became enveloped in clouds of smoke, and without warning burst as suddenly from roof and upper story into vivid flame. There were eye-witnesses who declared that a stream of living fire seemed to leap upon it from the burning district, and connected the space between them with an arch of luminous heat. In another instant the whole district was involved in a whirlwind of smoke and flame, out of whose seething vortex the corrugated iron buildings occasionally showed their shriveling or glowing outlines. And then the fire swept on and away.

When the sun again arose over the panic-stricken and devastated city, all personal incident and disaster was forgotten in the larger calamity. It was two or three days before the full particulars could be gathered—even while the dominant and resistless energy of the people was erecting new buildings upon the still-smoking ruins. It was only on the third day afterwards that James Farendell, on the deck of a coasting steamer, creeping out through the fogs of the Golden Gate, read the latest news in a San Francisco paper brought by the pilot. As he hurriedly comprehended the magnitude of the loss, which was far beyond his previous conception, he experienced a certain satisfaction in finding his position no worse materially than that of many of his fellow workers. THEY were ruined like himself; THEY must begin their life afresh—but then! Ah! there was still that terrible difference. He drew his breath quickly, and read on. Suddenly he stopped, transfixed by a later paragraph. For an instant he failed to grasp its full significance. Then he read it again, the words imprinting themselves on his senses with a slow deliberation that seemed to him as passionless as Scranton's utterances on that fateful night.

"The loss of life, it is now feared, is much greater than at first imagined. To the list that has been already published we must add the name of James Farendell, the energetic contractor so well known to our citizens, who was missing the morning after the fire. His calcined remains were found this afternoon in the warped and twisted iron shell of his counting-house, the wooden frame having been reduced to charcoal in the intense heat. The unfortunate man seems to have gone there to remove his books and papers,—as was evidenced by the iron safe being found open,—but to have been caught and imprisoned in the building through the heat causing the metal sheathing to hermetically seal the doors and windows. He was seen by some neighbors to enter the building while the fire was still distant, and his remains were identified by his keys, which were found beneath him. A poignant interest is added to his untimely fate by the circumstance that he was to have been married on the following day to the widow of his late partner, and that he had, at the call of duty, that very evening left a dinner party given to celebrate the last day of his bachelorhood—or, as it has indeed proved, of his earthly existence. Two families are thus placed in mourning, and it is a singular sequel that by this untoward calamity the well-known firm of Farendell & Cutler may be said to have ceased to exist."

Mr. Farendell started to his feet. But a lurch of the schooner as she rose on the long swell of the Pacific sent him staggering dizzily back to his seat, and checked his first wild impulse to return. He saw it all now,—the fire had avenged him by wiping out his persecutor, Scranton, but in the eyes of his contemporaries it had only erased HIM! He might return to refute the story in his own person, but the dead man's partner still lived with his secret, and his own rehabilitation could only revive his former peril.

*****

Four years elapsed before the late Mr. Farendell again set foot in the levee of Sacramento. The steamboat that brought him from San Francisco was a marvel to him in size, elegance, and comfort; so different from the little, crowded, tri-weekly packet he remembered; and it might, in a manner, have prepared him for the greater change in the city. But he was astounded to find nothing to remind him of the past,— no landmark, nor even ruin, of the place he had known.

Blocks of brick buildings, with thoroughfares having strange titles, occupied the district where his counting-house had stood, and even obliterated its site; equally strange names were upon the shops and warehouses. In his four years' wanderings he had scarcely found a place as unfamiliar. He had trusted to the great change in his own appearance—the full beard that he wore and the tanning of a tropical sun—to prevent recognition; but the precaution was unnecessary, there were none to recognize him in the new faces which were the only ones he saw in the transformed city. A cautious allusion to the past which he had made on the boat to a fellow passenger had brought only the surprised rejoinder, "Oh, that must have been before the big fire," as if it was an historic epoch. There was something of pain even in this assured security of his loneliness. His obliteration was complete.

For the late Mr. Farendell had suffered some change of mind with his other mutations. He had been singularly lucky. The schooner in which he had escaped brought him to Acapulco, where, as a returning Californian, and a presumably successful one, his services and experience were eagerly sought by an English party engaged in developing certain disused Mexican mines. As the post, however, was perilously near the route of regular emigration, as soon as he had gained a sufficient sum he embarked with some goods to Callao, where he presently established himself in business, resuming his REAL name—the unambitious but indistinctive one of "Smith." It is highly probable that this prudential act was also his first step towards rectitude. For whether the change was a question of moral ethics, or merely a super-stitious essay in luck, he was thereafter strictly honest in business. He became prosperous. He had been sustained in his flight by the intention that, if he were successful elsewhere, he would endeavor to communicate with his abandoned fiancee, and ask her to join him, and share not his name but fortune in exile. But as he grew rich, the difficulties of carrying out this intention became more apparent; he was by no means certain of her loyalty surviving the deceit he had practiced and the revelation he would have to make; he was doubtful of the success of any story which at other times he would have glibly invented to take the place of truth. Already several months had elapsed since his supposed death; could he expect her to be less accessible to premature advances now than when she had been a widow? Perhaps this made him think of the wife he had deserted so long ago. He had been quite content to live without regret or affection, forgetting and forgotten, but in his present prosperity he felt there was some need of putting his domestic affairs into a more secure and legitimate shape, to avert any catastrophe like the last. HERE at least would be no difficulty; husbands had deserted their wives before this in Californian emigration, and had been heard of only after they had made their fortune. Any plausible story would be accepted by HER in the joy of his reappearance; or if, indeed, as he reflected with equal complacency, she was dead or divorced from him through his desertion—a sufficient cause in her own State—and re-married, he would at least be more secure. He began, without committing himself, by inquiry and anonymous correspondence. His wife, he learnt, had left Missouri for Sacramento only a month or two after his own disappearance from that place, and her address was unknown!

A complication so unlooked for disquieted him, and yet whetted his curiosity. The only person she might meet in California who could possibly identify him with the late Mr. Farendell was Duffy; he had often wondered if that mysterious partner of Scranton's had been deceived with the others, or had ever suspected that the body discovered in the counting-house was Scranton's. If not, he must have accepted the strange coincidence that Scranton had disappeared also the same night. In the first six months of his exile he had searched the Californian papers thoroughly, but had found no record of any doubt having been thrown on the accepted belief. It was these circumstances, and perhaps a vague fascination not unlike that which impels the malefactor to haunt the scene of his crime, that, at the end of four years, had brought him, a man of middle age and assured occupation and fortune, back to the city he had fled from.

A few days at one of the new hotels convinced him thoroughly that he was in no danger of recognition, and gave him the assurance to take rooms more in keeping with his circumstances and his own frankly avowed position as the head of a South American house. A cautious acquaintance—through the agency of his banker—with a few business men gave him some occupation, and the fact of his South American letters being addressed to Don Diego Smith gave a foreign flavor to his individuality, which his tanned face and dark beard had materially helped. A stronger test convinced him how complete was the obliteration of his former identity. One day at the bank he was startled at being introduced by the manager to a man whom he at once recognized as a former business acquaintance. But the shock was his alone; the formal approach and unfamiliar manner of the man showed that he had failed to recognize even a resemblance. But would he equally escape detection by his wife if he met her as accidentally,—an encounter not to be thought of until he knew something more of her? He became more cautious in going to public places, but luckily for him the proportion of women to men was still small in California, and they were more observed than observing.

A month elapsed; in that time he had thoroughly exhausted the local Directories in his cautious researches among the "Smiths," for in his fear of precipitating a premature disclosure he had given up his former anonymous advertising. And there was a certain occupation in this personal quest that filled his business time. He was in no hurry. He had a singular faith that he would eventually discover her whereabouts, be able to make all necessary inquiries into her conduct and habits, and perhaps even enjoy a brief season of unsuspected personal observation before revealing himself. And this faith was as singularly rewarded.

Having occasion to get his watch repaired one day he entered a large jeweler's shop, and while waiting its examination his attention was attracted by an ordinary old-fashioned daguerreotype case in the form of a heart-shaped locket lying on the counter with other articles left for repairs. Something in its appearance touched a chord in his memory; he lifted the half-opened case and saw a much faded daguerreotype portrait of himself taken in Missouri before he left in the Californian emigration. He recognized it at once as one he had given to his wife; the faded likeness was so little like his present self that he boldly examined it and asked the jeweler one or two questions. The man was communicative. Yes, it was an old-fashioned affair which had been left for repairs a few days ago by a lady whose name and address, written by herself, were on the card tied to it.

Mr. James Smith had by this time fully controlled the emotion he felt as he recognized his wife's name and handwriting, and knew that at last the clue was found! He laid down the case carelessly, gave the final directions for the repairs of his watch, and left the shop. The address, of which he had taken a mental note, was, to his surprise, very near his own lodgings; but he went straight home. Here a few inquiries of his janitor elicited the information that the building indicated in the address was a large one of furnished apartments and offices like his own, and that the "Mrs. Smith" must be simply the housekeeper of the landlord, whose name appeared in the Directory, but not her own. Yet he waited until evening before he ventured to reconnoitre the premises; with the possession of his clue came a slight cooling of his ardor and extreme caution in his further proceedings. The house—a reconstructed wooden building—offered no external indication of the rooms she occupied in the uniformly curtained windows that front the street. Yet he felt an odd and pleasurable excitement in passing once or twice before those walls that hid the goal of his quest. As yet he had not seen her, and there was naturally the added zest of expectation. He noticed that there was a new building opposite, with vacant offices to let. A project suddenly occurred to him, which by morning he had fully matured. He hired a front room in the first floor of the new building, had it hurriedly furnished as a private office, and on the second morning of his discovery was installed behind his desk at the window commanding a full view of the opposite house. There was nothing strange in the South American capitalist selecting a private office in so popular a locality.

Two or three days elapsed without any result from his espionage. He came to know by sight the various tenants, the two Chinese servants, and the solitary Irish housemaid, but as yet had no glimpse of the housekeeper. She evidently led a secluded life among her duties; it occurred to him that perhaps she went out, possibly to market, earlier than he came, or later, after he had left the office. In this belief he arrived one morning after an early walk in a smart spring shower, the lingering straggler of the winter rains. There were few people astir, yet he had been preceded for two or three blocks by a tall woman whose umbrella partly concealed her head and shoulders from view. He had noticed, however, even in his abstraction, that she walked well, and managed the lifting of her skirt over her trim ankles and well-booted feet with some grace and cleverness. Yet it was only on her unexpectedly turning the corner of his own street that he became interested. She continued on until within a few doors of his office, when she stopped to give an order to a tradesman, who was just taking down his shutters. He heard her voice distinctly; in the quick emotion it gave him he brushed hurriedly past her without lifting his eyes. Gaining his own doorway he rushed upstairs to his office, hastily unlocked it, and ran to the window. The lady was already crossing the street. He saw her pause before the door of the opposite house, open it with a latchkey, and caught a full view of her profile in the single moment that she turned to furl her umbrella and enter. It was his wife's voice he had heard; it was his wife's face that he had seen in profile.

Yet she was changed from the lanky young schoolgirl he had wedded ten years ago, or, at least, compared to what his recollection of her had been. Had he ever seen her as she really was? Surely somewhere in that timid, freckled, half-grown bride he had known in the first year of their marriage the germ of this self-possessed, matured woman was hidden. There was the tone of her voice; he had never recalled it before as a lover might, yet now it touched him; her profile he certainly remembered, but not with the feeling it now produced in him. Would he have ever abandoned her had she been like that? Or had HE changed, and was this no longer his old self?—perhaps even a self SHE would never recognize again? James Smith had the superstitions of a gambler, and that vague idea of fate that comes to weak men; a sudden fright seized him, and he half withdrew from the window lest she should observe him, recognize him, and by some act precipitate that fate.

By lingering beyond the usual hour for his departure he saw her again, and had even a full view of her face as she crossed the street. The years had certainly improved her; he wondered with a certain nervousness if she would think they had done the same for him. The complacency with which he had at first contemplated her probable joy at recovering him had become seriously shaken since he had seen her; a woman as well preserved and good-looking as that, holding a certain responsible and, no doubt, lucrative position, must have many admirers and be independent. He longed to tell her now of his fortune, and yet shrank from the test its exposure implied. He waited for her return until darkness had gathered, and then went back to his lodgings a little chagrined and ill at ease. It was rather late for her to be out alone! After all, what did he know of her habits or associations? He recalled the freedom of Californian life, and the old scandals relating to the lapses of many women who had previously led blameless lives in the Atlantic States. Clearly it behooved him to be cautious. Yet he walked late that night before the house again, eager to see if she had returned, and with WHOM? He was restricted in his eagerness by the fear of detection, but he gathered very little knowledge of her habits; singularly enough nobody seemed to care. A little piqued at this, he began to wonder if he were not thinking too much of this woman to whom he still hesitated to reveal himself. Nevertheless, he found himself that night again wandering around the house, and even watching with some anxiety the shadow which he believed to be hers on the window-blind of the room where he had by discreet inquiry located her. Whether his memory was stimulated by his quest he never knew, but presently he was able to recall step by step and incident by incident his early courtship of her and the brief days of their married life. He even remembered the day she accepted him, and even dwelt upon it with a sentimental thrill that he probably never felt at the time, and it was a distinct feature of his extraordinary state of mind and its concentration upon this particular subject that he presently began to look upon HIMSELF as the abandoned and deserted conjugal partner, and to nurse a feeling of deep injury at her hands! The fact that he was thinking of her, and she, probably, contented with her lot, was undisturbed by any memory of him, seemed to him a logical deduction of his superior affection.

It was, therefore, quite as much in the attitude of a reproachful and avenging husband as of a merely curious one that, one afternoon, seeing her issue from her house at an early hour, he slipped down the stairs and began to follow her at a secure distance. She turned into the principal thoroughfare, and presently made one of the crowd who were entering a popular place of amusement where there was an afternoon performance. So complete was his selfish hallucination, that he smiled bitterly at this proof of heartless indifference, and even so far overcame his previous caution as to actually brush by her somewhat rudely as he entered the building at the same moment. He was conscious that she lifted her eyes a little impatiently to the face of the awkward stranger; he was equally, but more bitterly, conscious that she had not recognized him! He dropped into a seat behind her; she did not look at him again with even a sense of disturbance; the momentary contact had evidently left no impression upon her. She glanced casually at her neighbors on either side, and presently became absorbed in the performance. When it was over she rose, and on her way out recognized and exchanged a few words with one or two acquaintances. Again he heard her familiar voice, almost at his elbow, raised with no more consciousness of her contiguity to him than if he were a mere ghost. The thought struck him for the first time with a hideous and appalling significance. What was he but a ghost to her—to every one! A man dead, buried, and forgotten! His vanity and self-complacency vanished before this crushing realization of the hopelessness of his existence. Dazed and bewildered, he mingled blindly and blunderingly with the departing crowd, tossed here and there as if he were an invisible presence, stumbling over the impeding skirts of women with a vague apology they heeded not, and which seemed in his frightened ears as hollow as a voice from the grave.

When he at last reached the street he did not look back, but wandered abstractedly through by-streets in the falling rain, scarcely realizing where he was, until he found himself drenched through, with his closed umbrella in his tremulous hand, standing at the half-submerged levee beside the overflowed river. Here again he realized how completely he had been absorbed and concentrated in his search for his wife during the last three weeks; he had never been on the levee since his arrival. He had taken no note of the excitement of the citizens over the alarming reports of terrible floods in the mountains, and the daily and hourly fear that they experienced of disastrous inundation from the surcharged river. He had never thought of it, yet he had read of it, and even talked, and yet now for the first time in his selfish, blind absorption was certain of it. He stood still for some time, watching doggedly the enormous yellow stream laboring with its burden and drift from many a mountain town and camp, moving steadily and fatefully towards the distant bay, and still more distant and inevitable ocean. For a few moments it vaguely fascinated and diverted him; then it as vaguely lent itself to his one dominant, haunting thought. Yes, it was pointing him the only way out,—the path to the distant ocean and utter forgetfulness again!

The chill of his saturated clothing brought him to himself once more, he turned and hurried home. He went tiredly to his bedroom, and while changing his garments there came a knock at the door. It was the porter to say that a lady had called, and was waiting for him in the sitting-room. She had not given her name.

The closed door prevented the servant from seeing the extraordinary effect produced by this simple announcement upon the tenant. For one instant James Smith remained spellbound in his chair. It was characteristic of his weak nature and singular prepossession that he passed in an instant from the extreme of doubt to the extreme of certainty and conviction. It was his wife! She had recognized him in that moment of encounter at the entertainment; had found his address, and had followed him here! He dressed himself with feverish haste, not, however, without a certain care of his appearance and some selection of apparel, and quickly forecast the forthcoming interview in his mind. For the pendulum had swung back; Mr. James Smith was once more the self-satisfied, self-complacent, and discreetly cautious husband that he had been at the beginning of his quest, perhaps with a certain sense of grievance superadded. He should require the fullest explanations and guarantees before committing himself,—indeed, her present call might be an advance that it would be necessary for him to check. He even pictured her pleading at his feet; a very little stronger effort of his Alnaschar imagination would have made him reject her like the fatuous Persian glass peddler.

He opened the door of the sitting-room deliberately, and walked in with a certain formal precision. But the figure of a woman arose from the sofa, and with a slight outcry, half playful, half hysterical, threw herself upon his breast with the single exclamation, "Jim!" He started back from the double shock. For the woman was NOT his wife! A woman extravagantly dressed, still young, but bearing, even through her artificially heightened color, a face worn with excitement, excess, and premature age. Yet a face that as he disengaged himself from her arms grew upon him with a terrible recognition, a face that he had once thought pretty, inexperienced, and innocent,—the face of the widow of his former partner, Cutler, the woman he was to have married on the day he fled. The bitter revulsion of feeling and astonishment was evidently visible in his face, for she, too, drew back for a moment as they separated. But she had evidently been prepared, if not pathetically inured to such experiences. She dropped into a chair again with a dry laugh, and a hard metallic voice, as she said,—

"Well, it's YOU, anyway—and you can't get out of it."

As he still stared at her, in her inconsistent finery, draggled and wet by the storm, at her limp ribbons and ostentatious jewelry, she continued, in the same hard voice,—

"I thought I spotted you once or twice before; but you took no notice of me, and I reckoned I was mistaken. But this afternoon at the Temple of Music"—

"Where?" said James Smith harshly.

"At the Temple—the San Francisco Troupe performance—where you brushed by me, and I heard your voice saying, 'Beg pardon!' I says, 'That's Jim Farendell.'"

"Farendell!" burst out James Smith, half in simulated astonishment, half in real alarm.

"Well! Smith, then, if you like better," said the woman impatiently; "though it's about the sickest and most played-out dodge of a name you could have pitched upon. James Smith, Don Diego Smith!" she repeated, with a hysteric laugh. "Why, it beats the nigger minstrels all hollow! Well, when I saw you there, I said, 'That's Jim Farendell, or his twin brother;' I didn't say 'his ghost,' mind you; for, from the beginning, even before I knew it all, I never took any stock in that fool yarn about your burnt bones being found in your office."

"Knew all, knew what?" demanded the man, with a bravado which he nevertheless felt was hopeless.

She rose, crossed the room, and, standing before him, placed one hand upon her hip as she looked at him with half-pitying effrontery.

"Look here, Jim," she began slowly, "do you know what you're doing? Well, you're making me tired!" In spite of himself, a half-superstitious thrill went through him as her words and attitude recalled the dead Scranton. "Do you suppose that I don't know that you ran away the night of the fire? Do you suppose that I don't know that you were next to ruined that night, and that you took that opportunity of skedaddling out of the country with all the money you had left, and leaving folks to imagine you were burnt up with the books you had falsified and the accounts you had doctored! It was a mean thing for you to do to me, Jim, for I loved you then, and would have been fool enough to run off with you if you'd told me all, and not left me to find out that you had lost MY money—every cent Cutler had left me in the business—with the rest."

With the fatuousness of a weak man cornered, he clung to unimportant details. "But the body was believed to be mine by every one," he stammered angrily. "My papers and books were burnt,—there was no evidence."

"And why was there not?" she said witheringly, staring doggedly in his face. "Because I stopped it! Because when I knew those bones and rags shut up in that office weren't yours, and was beginning to make a row about it, a strange man came to me and said they were the remains of a friend of his who knew your bankruptcy and had come that night to warn you,—a man whom you had half ruined once, a man who had probably lost his life in helping you away. He said if I went on making a fuss he'd come out with the whole truth—how you were a thief and a forger, and"—she stopped.

"And what else?" he asked desperately, dreading to hear his wife's name next fall from her lips.

"And that—as it could be proved that his friend knew your secrets," she went on in a frightened, embarrassed voice, "you might be accused of making away with him."

For a moment James Smith was appalled; he had never thought of this. As in all his past villainy he was too cowardly to contemplate murder, he was frightened at the mere accusation of it. "But," he stammered, forgetful of all save this new terror, "he KNEW I wouldn't be such a fool, for the man himself told me Duffy had the papers, and killing him wouldn't have helped me."

Mrs. Cutler stared at him a moment searchingly, and then turned wearily away. "Well," she said, sinking into her chair again, "he said if I'd shut my mouth he'd shut his—and—I did. And this," she added, throwing her hands from her lap, a gesture half of reproach and half of contempt,—"this is what I get for it."

More frightened than touched by the woman's desperation, James Smith stammered a vague apologetic disclaimer, even while he was loathing with a revulsion new to him her draggled finery, her still more faded beauty, and the half-distinct consciousness of guilt that linked her to him. But she waved it away, a weary gesture that again reminded him of the dead Scranton.

"Of course I ain't what I was, but who's to blame for it? When you left me alone without a cent, face to face with a lie, I had to do something. I wasn't brought up to work; I like good clothes, and you know it better than anybody. I ain't one of your stage heroines that go out as dependants and governesses and die of consumption, but I thought," she went on with a shrill, hysterical laugh, more painful than the weariness which inevitably followed it, "I thought I might train myself to do it, ON THE STAGE! and I joined Barker's

Company. They said I had a face and figure for the stage; that face and figure wore out before I had anything more to show, and I wasn't big enough to make better terms with the manager. They kept me nearly a year doing chambermaids and fairy queens the other side of the footlights, where I saw you today. Then I kicked! I suppose I might have married some fool for his money, but I was soft enough to think you might be sending for me when you were safe. You seem to be mighty comfortable here," she continued, with a bitter glance around his handsomely furnished room, "as 'Don Diego Smith.' I reckon skedaddling pays better than staying behind."

"I have only been here a few weeks," he said hurriedly. "I never knew what had become of you, or that you were still here"—

"Or you wouldn't have come," she interrupted, with a bitter laugh. "Speak out, Jim."

"If there—is anything—I can do—for you," he stammered, "I'm sure"—

"Anything you can do?" she repeated, slowly and scornfully. "Anything you can do NOW? Yes!" she screamed, suddenly rising, crossing the room, and grasping his arms convulsively. "Yes! Take me away from here—anywhere—at once! Look, Jim," she went on feverishly, "let bygones be bygones —I won't peach! I won't tell on you—though I had it in my heart when you gave me the go-by just now! I'll do anything you say—go to your farthest hiding-place—work for you— only take me out of this cursed place."

Her passionate pleading stung even through his selfishness and loathing. He thought of his wife's indifference! Yes, he might be driven to this, and at least he must secure the only witness against his previous misconduct. "We will see," he said soothingly, gently loosening her hands. "We must talk it over." He stopped as his old suspiciousness returned. "But you must have some friends," he said searchingly, "some one who has helped you."

"None! Only one—he helped me at first," she hesitated—"Duffy."

"Duffy!" said James Smith, recoiling.

"Yes, when he had to tell me all," she said in half-frightened tones, "he was sorry for me. Listen, Jim! He was a square man, for all he was devoted to his partner—and you can't blame him for that. I think he helped me because I was alone; for nothing else, Jim. I swear it! He helped me from time to time. Maybe he might have wanted to marry me if he had not been waiting for another woman that he loved, a married woman that had been deserted years ago by her husband, just as you might have deserted me if we'd been married that day. He helped her and paid for her journey here to seek her husband, and set her up in business."

"What are you talking about—what woman?" stammered James Smith, with a strange presentiment creeping over him.

"A Mrs. Smith. Yes," she said quickly, as he started, "not a sham name like yours, but really and truly SMITH—that was her husband's name! I'm not lying, Jim," she went on, evidently mistaking the cause of the sudden contraction of the man's face. "I didn't invent her nor her name; there IS such a woman, and Duffy loves her—and HER only, and he never, NEVER was anything more than a friend to me. I swear it!"

The room seemed to swim around him. She was staring at

him, but he could see in her vacant eyes that she had no conception of his secret, nor knew the extent of her revelation. Duffy had not dared to tell all! He burst into a coarse laugh. "What matters Duffy or the silly woman he'd try to steal away from other men."

"But he didn't try to steal her, and she's only silly because she wants to be true to her husband while he lives. She told Duffy she'd never marry him until she saw her husband's dead face. More fool she," she added bitterly.

"Until she saw her husband's dead face," was all that James Smith heard of this speech. His wife's faithfulness through years of desertion, her long waiting and truthfulness, even the bitter commentary of the equally injured woman before him, were to him as nothing to what that single sentence conjured up. He laughed again, but this time strangely and vacantly. "Enough of this Duffy and his intrusion in my affairs until I'm able to settle my account with him. Come," he added brusquely, "if we are going to cut out of this at once I've got much to do. Come here again to-morrow, early. This Duffy—does he live here?"

"No. In Marysville."

"Good! Come early to-morrow."

As she seemed to hesitate, he opened a drawer of his table and took out a handful of gold, and handed it to her. She glanced at it for a moment with a strange expression, put it mechanically in her pocket, and then looking up at him said, with a forced laugh, "I suppose that means I am to clear out?"

"Until to-morrow," he said shortly.

"If the Sacramento don't sweep us away before then," she interrupted, with a reckless laugh; "the river's broken through the levee—a clear sweep in two places. Where I live the water's up to the doorstep. They say it's going to be the biggest flood yet. You're all right here; you're on higher ground."

She seemed to utter these sentences abstractedly, disconnectedly, as if to gain time. He made an impatient gesture.

"All right, I'm going," she said, compressing her lips slowly to keep them from trembling. "You haven't forgotten anything?" As he turned half angrily towards her she added, hurriedly and bitterly, "Anything—for to-morrow?"

"No!"

She opened the door and passed out. He listened until the trail of her wet skirt had descended the stairs, and the street door had closed behind her. Then he went back to his table and began collecting his papers and putting them away in his trunks, which he packed feverishly, yet with a set and determined face. He wrote one or two letters, which he sealed and left upon his table. He then went to his bedroom and deliberately shaved off his disguising beard. Had he not been so preoccupied in one thought, he might have been conscious of loud voices in the street and a hurrying of feet on the wet sidewalk. But he was possessed by only one idea. He must see his wife that evening! How, he knew not yet, but the way would appear when he had reached his office in the building opposite hers. Three hours had elapsed before he had finished his preparations. On going downstairs he stopped to give some directions to the porter, but his room was empty; passing into the street he was surprised to find it quite deserted, and the shops closed; even a drinking saloon at the corner was quite empty. He turned the corner of the street, and began the slight descent towards his office. To his amazement the lower end of the street, which was crossed by the thoroughfare which was his destination, was blocked by a crowd of people. As he hurried forward to join them he suddenly saw, moving down that thoroughfare, what appeared to his startled eyes to be the smokestacks of some small, flat-bottomed steamer. He rubbed his eyes; it was no illusion, for the next moment he had reached the crowd, who were standing half a block away from the thoroughfare, and on the edge of a lagoon of yellow water, whose main current was the thoroughfare he was seeking, and between whose houses, submerged to their first stories, a steamboat was really paddling. Other boats and rafts were adrift on its sluggish waters, and a boatman had just landed a passenger in the backwater of the lower half of the street on which he stood with the crowd.

Possessed of his one idea, he fought his way desperately to the water edge and the boat, and demanded a passage to his office. The boatman hesitated, but James Smith promptly offered him double the value of his craft. The act was not deemed singular in that extravagant epoch, and the sympathizing crowd cheered his solitary departure, as he declined even the services of the boatman. The next moment he was off in mid-stream of the thoroughfare, paddling his boat with a desperate but inexperienced hand until he reached his office, which he entered by the window. The building, which was new and of brick, showed very little damage from the flood, but in far different case was the one opposite, on which his eyes were eagerly bent, and whose cheap and insecure foundations he could see the flood was already undermining. There were boats around the house, and men hurriedly removing trunks and valuables, but the one figure he expected to see was not there. He tied his own boat to the window; there was evidently no chance of an interview now, but if she were leaving there would be still the chance of following her and knowing her destination. As he gazed she suddenly appeared at a window, and was helped by a boatman into a flat-bottomed barge containing trunks and furniture. She was evidently the last to leave. The other boats put off at once, and none too soon; for there was a warning cry, a quick swerving of the barge, and the end of the dwelling slowly dropped into the flood, seeming to sink on its knees like a stricken ox. A great undulation of yellow water swept across the street, inundating his office through the open window and half swamping his boat beside it. At the same time he could see that the current had changed and increased in volume and velocity, and, from the cries and warning of the boatmen, he knew that the river had burst its banks at its upper bend. He had barely time to leap into his boat and cast it off before there was a foot of water on his floor.

But the new current was carrying the boats away from the higher level, which they had been eagerly seeking, and towards the channel of the swollen river. The barge was first to feel its influence, and was hurried towards the river against the strongest efforts of its boatmen. One by one the other and smaller boats contrived to get into the slack water of crossing streets, and one was swamped before his eyes. But James Smith kept only the barge in view. His difficulty in following it was increased by his inexperience in managing a boat, and the quantity of drift which now charged the current. Trees torn by their roots from some upland bank; sheds, logs, timber, and the bloated carcasses of cattle choked the stream. All the ruin worked by the flood seemed to be compressed in this disastrous current. Once or twice he narrowly escaped collision with a heavy beam or the bed of some farmer's wagon. Once he was swamped by a tree, and righted his frail boat while clinging to its branches.

And then those who watched him from the barge and shore

said afterwards that a great apathy seemed to fall upon him. He no longer attempted to guide the boat or struggle with the drift, but sat in the stern with intent forward gaze and motionless paddles. Once they strove to warn him, called to him to make an effort to reach the barge, and did what they could, in spite of their own peril, to alter their course and help him. But he neither answered nor heeded them. And then suddenly a great log that they had just escaped seemed to rise up under the keel of his boat, and it was gone. After a moment his face and head appeared above the current, and so close to the stern of the barge that there was a slight cry from the woman in it, but the next moment, and before the boatman could reach him, he was drawn under it and disappeared. They lay on their oars eagerly watching, but the body of James Smith was sucked under the barge, and, in the mid-channel of the great river, was carried out towards the distant sea.

*****

There was a strange meeting that night on the deck of a relief boat, which had been sent out in search of the missing barge, between Mrs. Smith and a grave and anxious passenger who had chartered it. When he had comforted her, and pointed out, as, indeed, he had many times before, the loneliness and insecurity of her unprotected life, she yielded to his arguments. But it was not until many months after their marriage that she confessed to him on that eventful night she thought she had seen in a moment of great peril the vision of the dead face of her husband uplifted to her through the water.

LANTY FOSTER'S MISTAKE

Lanty Foster was crouching on a low stool before the dying kitchen fire, the better to get its fading radiance on the book she was reading. Beyond, through the open window and door, the fire was also slowly fading from the sky and the mountain ridge whence the sun had dropped half an hour before. The view was uphill, and the sky-line of the hill was marked by two or three gibbet-like poles from which, on a now invisible line between them, depended certain objects—mere black silhouettes against the sky—which bore weird likeness to human figures. Absorbed as she was in her book, she nevertheless occasionally cast an impatient glance in that direction, as the sunlight faded more quickly than her fire. For the fluttering objects were the "week's wash" which had to be brought in before night fell and the mountain wind arose. It was strong at that altitude, and before this had ravished the clothes from the line, and scattered them along the highroad leading over the ridge, once even lashing the shy schoolmaster with a pair of Lanty's own stockings, and blinding the parson with a really tempestuous petticoat.

A whiff of wind down the big-throated chimney stirred the log embers on the hearth, and the girl jumped to her feet, closing the book with an impatient snap. She knew her mother's voice would follow. It was hard to leave her heroine at the crucial moment of receiving an explanation from a presumed faithless lover, just to climb a hill and take in a lot of soulless washing, but such are the infelicities of stolen romance reading. She threw the clothes-basket over her head like a hood, the handle resting across her bosom and shoulders, and with both her hands free started out of the cabin. But the darkness had come up from the valley in one stride after its mountain fashion, had outstripped her, and she was instantly plunged in it. Still the outline of the ridge above her was visible, with the white, steadfast stars that were not there a moment ago, and by that sign she knew she was late. She had to battle against the rushing wind now, which sung through the inverted basket over her head and held her back, but with bent shoulders she at last reached the top of the ridge and the level. Yet here, owing to the shifting of the lighter background above her, she now found herself again encompassed with the darkness. The outlines of the poles had disappeared, the white fluttering garments were distinct apparitions waving in the wind, like dancing ghosts. But there certainly was a queer misshapen bulk moving beyond, which she did not recognize, and as she at last reached one of the poles, a shock was communicated to it, through the clothes-line and the bulk beyond. Then she heard a voice say impatiently,—

"What in h-ll am I running into now?"

It was a man's voice, and, from its elevation, the voice of a man on horseback. She answered without fear and with slow deliberation,—

"Inter our clothes-line, I reckon."

"Oh!" said the man in a half-apologetic tone. Then in brisker accents, "The very thing I want! I say, can you give me a bit of it? The ring of my saddle girth has fetched loose. I can fasten it with that."

"I reckon," replied Lanty, with the same unconcern, moving nearer the bulk, which now separated into two parts as the man dismounted. "How much do you want?"

"A foot or two will do."

They were now in front of each other, although their faces were not distinguishable to either. Lanty, who had been following the lines with her hand, here came upon the end knotted around the last pole. This she began to untie.

"What a place to hang clothes," he said curiously.

"Mighty dryin', tho'," returned Lanty laconically.

"And your house? Is it near by?" he continued.

"Just down the ridge—ye kin see from the edge. Got a knife?" She had untied the knot.

"No—yes—wait." He had hesitated a moment and then produced something from his breast pocket, which he however kept in his hand. As he did not offer it to her she simply held out a section of the rope between her hands, which he divided with a single cut. She saw only that the instrument was long and keen. Then she lifted the flap of the saddle for him as he attempted to fasten the loose ring with the rope, but the darkness made it impossible. With an ejaculation, he fumbled in his pockets. "My last match!" he said, striking it, as he crouched over it to protect it from the wind. Lanty leaned over also, with her apron raised between it and the blast. The flame for an instant lit up the ring, the man's dark face, mustache, and white teeth set together as he tugged at the girth, and Lanty's brown, velvet eyes and soft, round cheek framed in the basket. Then it went out, but the ring was secured.

"Thank you," said the man, with a short laugh, "but I thought you were a humpbacked witch in the dark there."

"And I couldn't make out whether you was a cow or a b'ar," returned the young girl simply.

Here, however, he quickly mounted his horse, but in the action something slipped from his clothes, struck a stone, and bounded away into the darkness.

"My knife," he said hurriedly. "Please hand it to me." But although the girl dropped on her knees and searched the ground diligently, it could not be found. The man with a restrained ejaculation again dismounted, and joined in the search.

"Haven't you got another match?" suggested Lanty.

"No—it was my last!" he said impatiently.

"Just you hol' on here," she said suddenly, "and I'll run down to the kitchen and fetch you a light. I won't be long."

"No! no!" said the man quickly; "don't! I couldn't wait. I've been here too long now. Look here. You come in daylight and find it, and—just keep it for me, will you?" He laughed. "I'll come for it. And now, if you'll only help to set me on that road again, for it's so infernal black I can't see the mare's ears ahead of me, I won't bother you any more. Thank you."

Lanty had quietly moved to his horse's head and taken the bridle in her hand, and at once seemed to be lost in the gloom. But in a few moments he felt the muffled thud of his horse's hoof on the thick dust of the highway, and its still hot, impalpable powder rising to his nostrils.

"Thank you," he said again, "I'm all right now," and in the pause that followed it seemed to Lanty that he had extended a parting hand to her in the darkness. She put up her own to meet it, but missed his, which had blundered onto her shoulder. Before she could grasp it, she felt him stooping over her, the light brush of his soft mustache on her cheek, and then the starting forward of his horse. But the retaliating box on the ear she had promptly aimed at him spent itself in the black space which seemed suddenly to have swallowed up the man, and even his light laugh.

For an instant she stood still, and then, swinging the basket indignantly from her shoulder, took up her suspended task. It was no light one in the increasing wind, and the unfastened clothes-line had precipitated a part of its burden to the ground through the loosening of the rope. But on picking up the trailing garments her hand struck an unfamiliar object. The stranger's lost knife! She thrust it hastily into the bottom of the basket and completed her work. As she began to descend with her burden she saw that the light of the kitchen fire, seen through the windows, was augmented by a candle. Her mother was evidently awaiting her.

"Pretty time to be fetchin' in the wash," said Mrs. Foster querulously. "But what can you expect when folks stand gossipin' and philanderin' on the ridge instead o' tendin' to their work?"

Now Lanty knew that she had NOT been "gossipin'" nor "philanderin'," yet as the parting salute might have been open to that imputation, and as she surmised that her mother might have overheard their voices, she briefly said, to prevent further questioning, that she had shown a stranger the road. But for her mother's unjust accusation she would have been more communicative. As Mrs. Foster went back grumblingly into the sitting-room Lanty resolved to keep the knife at present a secret from her mother, and to that purpose removed it from the basket. But in the light of the candle she saw it for the first time plainly—and started.

For it was really a dagger! jeweled-handled and richly wrought—such as Lanty had never looked upon before. The hilt was studded with gems, and the blade, which had a cutting edge, was damascened in blue and gold. Her soft eyes reflected the brilliant setting, her lips parted breathlessly; then, as her mother's voice arose in the other room, she thrust it back into its velvet sheath and clapped it into her pocket. Its rare beauty had confirmed her resolution of absolute secrecy. To have shown it now would have made "no end of talk." And she was not sure but that her parents would have demanded its custody! And it was given to HER by HIM to keep. This settled the question of moral ethics. She took the first opportunity to run up to her bedroom and hide it under the mattress.

Yet the thought of it filled the rest of her evening. When her household duties were done she took up her novel again, partly from force of habit and partly as an attitude in which she could think of IT undisturbed. For what was fiction to her now? True, it possessed a certain reminiscent value. A "dagger" had appeared in several romances she had devoured, but she never had a clear idea of one before. "The Count sprang back, and, drawing from his belt a richly jeweled dagger, hissed between his teeth," or, more to the purpose: "'Take this,' said Orlando, handing her the ruby-hilted poignard which had gleamed upon his thigh, 'and should the caitiff attempt thy unguarded innocence—'"

"Did ye hear what your father was sayin'?" Lanty started. It was her mother's voice in the doorway, and she had been vaguely conscious of another voice pitched in the same querulous key, which, indeed, was the dominant expression of the small ranchers of that fertile neighborhood. Possibly a too complaisant and unaggressive Nature had spoiled them.

"Yes!—no!" said Lanty abstractedly, "what did he say?"

"If you wasn't taken up with that fool book," said Mrs. Foster, glancing at her daughter's slightly conscious color, "ye'd know! He allowed ye'd better not leave yer filly in the far pasture nights. That gang o' Mexican horse-thieves is out again, and raided McKinnon's stock last night."

This touched Lanty closely. The filly was her own property, and she was breaking it for her own riding. But her distrust of her parents' interference was greater than any fear of horse-stealers. "She's mighty uneasy in the barn; and," she added, with a proud consciousness of that beautiful yet carnal weapon upstairs, "I reckon I ken protect her and myself agin any Mexican horse-thieves."

"My! but we're gettin' high and mighty," responded Mrs. Foster, with deep irony. "Did you git all that outer your fool book?"

"Mebbe," said Lanty curtly.

Nevertheless, her thoughts that night were not entirely based on written romance. She wondered if the stranger knew that she had really tried to box his ears in the darkness, also if he had been able to see her face. HIS she remembered, at least the flash of his white teeth against his dark face and darker mustache, which was quite as soft as her own hair. But if he thought "for a minnit" that she was "goin' to allow an entire stranger to kiss her—he was mighty mistaken." She should let him know it "pretty quick"! She should hand him back the dagger "quite careless like," and never let on that she'd thought anything of it. Perhaps that was the reason why, before she went to bed, she took a good look at it, and after taking off her straight, beltless, calico gown she even tried the effect of it, thrust in the stiff waistband of her petticoat, with the jeweled hilt displayed, and thought it looked charming—as indeed it did. And then, having said her prayers like a good girl, and supplicated that she should be less "tetchy" with her parents, she went to sleep and dreamed that she had gone out to take in the wash again, but that the clothes had all changed to the queerest lot of folks, who were all fighting and struggling with each other until she, Lanty, drawing her dagger, rushed up single-handed among them, crying, "Disperse, ye craven curs,—disperse, I say." And they dispersed.

Yet even Lanty was obliged to admit the next morning that all this was somewhat incongruous with the baking of "corn dodgers," the frying of fish, the making of beds, and her other household duties, and dismissed the stranger from her mind until he should "happen along." In her freer and more acceptable outdoor duties she even tolerated the advances of neighboring swains who made a point of passing by "Foster's Ranch," and who were quite aware that Atalanta Foster, alias "Lanty," was one of the prettiest girls in the country. But Lanty's toleration consisted in that singular performance known to herself as "giving them as good as they sent," being a lazy traversing, qualified with scorn, of all that they advanced. How long they would have put up with this from a plain girl I do not know, but Lanty's short upper lip seemed framed for indolent and fascinating scorn, and her dreamy eyes usually looked beyond the questioner, or blunted his bolder glances in their velvety surfaces. The libretto of these scenes was not exhaustive, e.g.:—

The Swain (with bold, bad gayety). "Saw that shy school-master hangin' round your ridge yesterday! Orter know by this time that shyness with a gal don't pay."

Bret Harte

Lanty (decisively). "Mebbe he allows it don't get left as often as impudence."

The Swain (ignoring the reply and his previous attitude and becoming more direct). "I was calkilatin' to say that with these yer hoss-thieves about, yer filly ain't safe in the pasture. I took a turn round there two or three times last evening to see if she was all right."

Lanty (with a flattering show of interest). "No! DID ye, now? I was jest wonderin'"—

The Swain (eagerly). "I did—quite late, too! Why, that's nothin', Miss Atalanty, to what I'd do for you."

Lanty (musing, with far off-eyes). "Then that's why she was so awful skeerd and frightened! Just jumpin' outer her skin with horror. I reckoned it was a b'ar or panther or a spook! You ought to have waited till she got accustomed to your looks."

Nevertheless, despite this elegant raillery, Lanty was enough concerned in the safety of her horse to visit it the next day with a view of bringing it nearer home. She had just stepped into the alder fringe of a dry "run" when she came suddenly upon the figure of a horseman in the "run," who had been hidden by the alders from the plain beyond and who seemed to be engaged in examining the hoof marks in the dust of the old ford. Something about his figure struck her recollection, and as he looked up quickly she saw it was the owner of the dagger. But he appeared to be lighter of hair and complexion, and was dressed differently, and more like a vaquero. Yet there was the same flash of his teeth as he recognized her, and she knew it was the same man.

Alas for her preparation! Without the knife she could not

make that haughty return of it which she had contemplated. And more than that, she was conscious she was blushing! Nevertheless she managed to level her pretty brown eyebrows at him, and said sharply that if he followed her to her home she would return his property at once.

"But I'm in no hurry for it," he said with a laugh,—the same light laugh and pleasant voice she remembered,—"and I'd rather not come to the house just now. The knife is in good hands, I know, and I'll call for it when I want it! And until then—if it's all the same to you—keep it to yourself,—keep it dark, as dark as the night I lost it!"

"I don't go about blabbing my affairs," said Lanty indignantly, "and if it hadn't BEEN dark that night you'd have had your ears boxed—you know why!"

The stranger laughed again, waved his hand to Lanty, and galloped away.

Lanty was a little disappointed. The daylight had taken away some of her illusions. He was certainly very good-looking, but not quite as picturesque, mysterious, and thrilling as in the dark! And it was very queer—he certainly did look darker that night! Who was he? And why was he lingering near her? He was different from her neighbors—her admirers. He might be one of those locaters, from the big towns, who prospect the lands, with a view of settling government warrants on them,—they were always so secret until they had found what they wanted. She did not dare to seek information of her friends, for the same reason that she had concealed his existence from her mother,—it would provoke awkward questions; and it was evident that he was trusting to her secrecy, too. The thought thrilled her with a new pride, and was some compensation for the loss of her more intangible romance. It would be mighty fine, when he did call openly for his beautiful knife and declared himself, to have them all know that SHE knew about it all along.

When she reached home, to guard against another such surprise she determined to keep the weapon with her, and, distrusting her pocket, confided it to the cheap little country-made corset which only for the last year had confined her budding figure, and which now, perhaps, heaved with an additional pride. She was quite abstracted during the rest of the day, and paid but little attention to the gossip of the farm lads, who were full of a daring raid, two nights before, by the Mexican gang on the large stock farm of a neighbor. The Vigilant Committee had been baffled; it was even alleged that some of the smaller ranchmen and herders were in league with the gang. It was also believed to be a widespread conspiracy; to have a political complexion in its combination of an alien race with Southwestern filibusters. The legal authorities had been reinforced by special detectives from San Francisco. Lanty seldom troubled herself with these matters; she knew the exaggeration, she suspected the ignorance of her rural neighbors. She roughly referred it, in her own vocabulary, to "jaw," a peculiarly masculine quality. But later in the evening, when the domestic circle in the sitting-room had been augmented by a neighbor, and Lanty had taken refuge behind her novel as an excuse for silence, Zob Hopper, the enamored swain of the previous evening, burst in with more astounding news. A posse of the sheriff had just passed along the ridge; they had "corraled" part of the gang, and rescued some of the stock. The leader of the gang had escaped, but his capture was inevitable, as the roads were stopped. "All the same, I'm glad to see ye took my advice, Miss Atalanty, and brought in your filly," he concluded, with an insinuating glance at the young girl.

But "Miss Atalanty," curling a quarter of an inch of scarlet lip above the edge of her novel, here "allowed" that if his advice or the filly had to be "took," she didn't know which was worse.

"I wonder ye kin talk to sech peartness, Mr. Hopper," said Mrs. Foster severely; "she ain't got eyes nor senses for anythin' but that book."

"Talkin' o' what's to be 'took,'" put in the diplomatic neighbor, "you bet it ain't that Mexican leader! No, sir! he's been 'stopped' before this—and then got clean away all the same! One o' them detectives got him once and disarmed him—but he managed to give them the slip, after all. Why, he's that full o' shifts and disguises thar ain't no spottin' him. He walked right under the constable's nose oncet, and took a drink with the sheriff that was arter him—and the blamed fool never knew it. He kin change even the color of his hair quick as winkin'."

"Is he a real Mexican,—a regular Greaser?" asked the paternal Foster. "Cos I never heard that they wuz smart."

"No! They say he comes o' old Spanish stock, a bad egg they threw outer the nest, I reckon," put in Hopper eagerly, seeing a strange animated interest dilating Lanty's eyes, and hoping to share in it; "but he's reg'lar high-toned, you bet! Why, I knew a man who seed him in his own camp—prinked out in a velvet jacket and silk sash, with gold chains and buttons down his wide pants and a dagger stuck in his sash, with a handle just blazin' with jew'ls. Yes! Miss Atalanty, they say that one stone at the top—a green stone, what they call an 'em'ral'—was worth the price o' a 'Frisco house-lot. True ez you live! Eh—what's up now?"

Lanty's book had fallen on the floor as she was rising to her feet with a white face, still more strange and distorted in an affected yawn behind her little hand. "Yer makin' me that sick and nervous with yer fool yarns," she said hysterically, "that I'm goin' to get a little fresh air. It's just stifling here with lies and terbacker!" With another high laugh, she brushed past him into the kitchen, opened the door, and then paused, and, turning, ran rapidly up to her bedroom. Here she locked herself in, tore open the bosom of her dress, plucked out the dagger, threw it on the bed, where the green stone gleamed for an instant in the candlelight, and then dropped on her knees beside the bed with her whirling head buried in her cold red hands.

It had all come to her in a flash, like a blaze of lightning,—the black, haunting figure on the ridge, the broken saddle girth, the abandonment of the dagger in the exigencies of flight and concealment; the second meeting, the skulking in the dry, alder-hidden "run," the changed dress, the lighter-colored hair, but always the same voice and laugh—the leader, the fugitive, the Mexican horse-thief! And she, the Godforsaken fool, the chuckle-headed nigger baby, with not half the sense of her own filly or that sop-headed Hopper—had never seen it! She—SHE who would be the laughing-stock of them all—she had thought him a "locater," a "towny" from 'Frisco! And she had consented to keep his knife until he would call for it,— yes, call for it, with fire and flame perhaps, the trampling of hoofs, pistol shots—and—yet—

Yet!—he had TRUSTED her. Yes! trusted her when he knew a word from her lips would have brought the whole district down on him! when the mere exposure of that dagger would have identified and damned him! Trusted her a second time, when she was within cry of her house! When he might have taken her filly without her knowing it? And now she remembered vaguely that the neighbors had said how strange it was that her father's stock had not suffered as theirs had. HE had protected them—he who was now a fugitive—and their men pursuing him! She rose suddenly with a single stamp of her narrow foot, and as suddenly became cool and sane. And then, quite her old self again, she lazily picked up the dagger and restored it to its place in her bosom. That done, with her color back and her eyes a little brighter, she deliberately went downstairs again, stuck her little brown head into the sitting-room, said cheerfully, "Still yawpin', you folks," and quietly passed out into the darkness.

She ran swiftly up to the ridge, impelled by the blind memory of having met him there at night and the one vague thought to give him warning. But it was dark and empty, with no sound but the rushing wind. And then an idea seized her. If he were haunting the vicinity still, he might see the fluttering of the clothes upon the line and believe she was there. She stooped quickly, and in the merciful and exonerating darkness stripped off her only white petticoat and pinned it on the line. It flapped, fluttered, and streamed in the mountain wind. She lingered and listened. But there came a sound she had not counted on,—the clattering hoofs of not ONE, but many, horses on the lower road! She ran back to the house to find its inmates already hastening towards the road for news. She took that chance to slip in quietly, go to her room, whose window commanded a view of the ridge, and crouching low behind it she listened. She could hear the sound of voices, and the dull trampling of heavy boots on the dusty path towards the barnyard on the other side of the house—a pause, and then the return of the trampling boots, and the final clattering of hoofs on the road again. Then there was a tap on her door and her mother's querulous voice.

"Oh! yer there, are ye? Well—it's the best place fer a girl—with all these man's doin's goin' on! They've got that Mexican horse-thief and have tied him up in your filly's stall in the barn—till the 'Frisco deputy gets back from rounding up the others. So ye jest stay where ye are till they've come

Bret Harte

and gone, and we're shut o' all that cattle. Are ye mindin'?"

"All right, maw; 'taint no call o' mine, anyhow," returned Lanty, through the half-open door.

At another time her mother might have been startled at her passive obedience. Still more would she have been startled had she seen her daughter's face now, behind the closed door—with her little mouth set over her clenched teeth. And yet it was her own child, and Lanty was her mother's real daughter; the same pioneer blood filled their veins, the blood that had never nourished cravens or degenerates, but had given itself to sprinkle and fertilize desert solitudes where man might follow. Small wonder, then, that this frontier-born Lanty, whose first infant cry had been answered by the yelp of wolf and scream of panther; whose father's rifle had been leveled across her cradle to cover the stealthy Indian who prowled outside, small wonder that she should feel herself equal to these "man's doin's," and prompt to take a part. For even in the first shock of the news of the capture she recalled the fact that the barn was old and rotten, that only that day the filly had kicked a board loose from behind her stall, which she, Lanty, had lightly returned to avoid "making a fuss." If his captors had not noticed it, or trusted only to their guards, she might make the opening wide enough to free him!

Two hours later the guard nearest the now sleeping house, a farm hand of the Fosters', saw his employer's daughter slip out and cautiously approach him. A devoted slave of Lanty's, and familiar with her impulses, he guessed her curiosity, and was not averse to satisfy it and the sense of his own importance. To her whispers of affected, half-terrified interest, he responded in whispers that the captive was really in the filly's stall, securely bound by his wrists behind his back, and his feet "hobbled" to a post. That Lanty couldn't see him, for it was dark inside, and he was sitting with his back to the wall, as he couldn't sleep comf'ble lyin' down. Lanty's eyes glowed, but her face was turned aside.

"And ye ain't reckonin' his friends will come and rescue him?" said Lanty, gazing with affected fearfulness in the darkness.

"Not much! There's two other guards down in the corral, and I'd fire my gun and bring 'em up."

But Lanty was gazing open-mouthed towards the ridge. "What's that wavin' on the ridge?" she said in awe-stricken tones.

She was pointing to the petticoat,—a vague, distant, moving object against the horizon.

"Why, that's some o' the wash on the line, ain't it?"

"Wash—TWO DAYS IN THE WEEK!" said Lanty sharply. "Wot's gone of you?"

"Thet's so," muttered the man, "and it wan't there at sundown, I'll swear! P'r'aps I'd better call the guard," and he raised his rifle.

"Don't," said Lanty, catching his arm. "Suppose it's nothin', they'll laugh at ye. Creep up softly and see; ye ain't afraid, are ye? If ye are, give me yer gun, and I'LL go."

This settled the question, as Lanty expected. The man cocked his piece, and bending low began cautiously to mount the acclivity. Lanty waited until his figure began to fade, and then ran like fire to the barn.

She had arranged every detail of her plan beforehand.

Crouching beside the wall of the stall she hissed through a crack in thrilling whispers, "Don't move. Don't speak for your life's sake. Wait till I hand you back your knife, then do the best you can." Then slipping aside the loosened board she saw dimly the black outline of curling hair, back, shoulders, and tied wrists of the captive. Drawing the knife from her pocket, with two strokes of its keen cutting edge she severed the cords, threw the knife into the opening, and darted away. Yet in that moment she knew that the man was instinctively turning towards her. But it was one thing to free a horse-thief, and another to stop and "philander" with him.

She ran halfway up the ridge, and met the farm hand returning. It was only a bit of washing after all, and he was glad he hadn't fired his gun. On the other hand, Lanty confessed she had got "so skeert" being alone, that she came to seek him. She had the shivers; wasn't her hand cold? It was, but thrilling even in its coldness to the bashfully admiring man. And she was that weak and dizzy, he must let her lean on his arm going down; and they must go SLOW. She was sure he was cold, too, and if he would wait at the back door she would give him a drink of whiskey. Thus Lanty, with her brain afire, her eyes and ears straining into the darkness, and the vague outline of the barn beyond. Another moment was protracted over the drink of whiskey, and then Lanty, with a faint archness, made him promise not to tell her mother of her escapade, and she promised on her part not to say anything about his "stalking a petticoat on the clothesline," and then shyly closed the door and regained her room. HE must have got away by this time, or have been discovered; she believed they would not open the barn door until the return of the posse.

She was right. It was near daybreak when they returned, and, again crouching low beside her window, she heard, with a fierce joy, the sudden outcry, the oaths, the wrangling voices, the summoning of her father to the front door, and then the tumultuous sweeping away again of the whole posse, and a blessed silence falling over the rancho. And then Lanty went quietly to bed, and slept like a three-year child!

Perhaps that was the reason why she was able at breakfast to listen with lazy and even rosy indifference to the startling events of the night; to the sneers of the farm hands at the posse who had overlooked the knife when they searched their prisoner, as well as the stupidity of the corral guard who had never heard him make a hole "the size of a house" in the barn side! Once she glanced demurely at Silas Briggs—the farm hand and the poor fellow felt consoled in his shame at the remembrance of their confidences.

But Lanty's tranquillity was not destined to last long. There was again the irruption of exciting news from the highroad; the Mexican leader had been recaptured, and was now safely lodged in Brownsville jail! Those who were previously loud in their praises of the successful horse-thief who had baffled the vigilance of his pursuers were now equally keen in their admiration of the new San Francisco deputy who, in turn, had outwitted the whole gang. It was HE who was fertile in expedients; HE who had studied the whole country, and even risked his life among the gang, and HE who had again closed the meshes of the net around the escaped outlaw. He was already returning by way of the rancho, and might stop there a moment,—so that they could all see the hero. Such was the power of success on the country-side! Outwardly indifferent, inwardly bitter, Lanty turned away. She should not grace his triumph, if she kept in her room all day! And when there was a clatter of hoofs on the road again, Lanty slipped upstairs.

But in a few moments she was summoned. Captain Lance Wetherby, Assistant Chief of Police of San Francisco, Deputy Sheriff and ex-U. S. scout, had requested to see Miss

Foster a few moments alone. Lanty knew what it meant,—her secret had been discovered; but she was not the girl to shirk the responsibility! She lifted her little brown head proudly, and with the same resolute step with which she had left the house the night before, descended the stairs and entered the sitting-room. At first she saw nothing. Then a remembered voice struck her ear; she started, looked up, and gasping, fell back against the door. It was the stranger who had given her the dagger, the stranger she had met in the run!—the horse-thief himself! No! no! she saw it all now—she had cut loose the wrong man!

He looked at her with a smile of sadness—as he drew from his breast-pocket that dreadful dagger, the very sight of which Lanty now loathed! "This is the SECOND time, Miss Foster," he said gently, "that I have taken this knife from Murietta, the Mexican bandit: once when I disarmed him three weeks ago, and he escaped, and last night, when he had again escaped and I recaptured him. After I lost it that night I understood from you that you had found it and were keeping it for me." He paused a moment and went on: "I don't ask you what happened last night. I don't condemn you for it; I can believe what a girl of your courage and sympathy might rightly do if her pity were excited; I only ask—why did you give HIM back that knife I trusted you with?"

"Why? Why did I?" burst out Lanty in a daring gush of truth, scorn, and temper. "BECAUSE I THOUGHT YOU WERE THAT HORSE-THIEF. There!"

He drew back astonished, and then suddenly came that laugh that Lanty remembered and now hailed with joy. "I believe you, by Jove!" he gasped. "That first night I wore the disguise in which I have tracked him and mingled with his gang. Yes! I see it all now—and more. I see that to YOU I owe his recapture!"

"To me!" echoed the bewildered girl; "how?"

"Why, instead of making for his cave he lingered here in the confines of the ranch! He thought you were in love with him, because you freed him and gave him his knife, and stayed to see you!"

But Lanty had her apron to her eyes, whose first tears were filling their velvet depths. And her voice was broken as she said,—

"Then he—cared—a—good deal more for me—than some people!"

But there is every reason to believe that Lanty was wrong! At least later events that are part of the history of Foster's Rancho and the Foster family pointed distinctly to the contrary.

Bret Harte

AN ALI BABA OF THE SIERRAS

Johnny Starleigh found himself again late for school. It was always happening. It seemed to be inevitable with the process of going to school at all. And it was no fault "o' his." Something was always occurring,—some eccentricity of Nature or circumstance was invariably starting up in his daily path to the schoolroom. He may not have been "thinkin' of squirrels," and yet the rarest and most evasive of that species were always crossing his trail; he may not have been "huntin' honey," and yet a wild bees' nest in the hollow of an oak absolutely obtruded itself before him; he wasn't "bird-catchin'," and yet there was a yellow-hammer always within stone's throw. He had heard how grown men hunters always saw the most wonderful animals when they "hadn't got a gun with 'em," and it seemed to be his lot to meet them in his restricted possibilities on the way to school. If Nature was thus capricious with his elders, why should folk think it strange if she was as mischievous with a small boy?

On this particular morning Johnny had been beguiled by the unmistakable footprints—so like his own!—of a bear's cub. What chances he had of ever coming up with them, or what he would have done if he had, he did not know. He only knew that at the end of an hour and a half he found himself two miles from the schoolhouse, and, from the position of the sun, at least an hour too late for school. He knew that nobody would believe him. The punishment for complete truancy was little worse than for being late. He resolved to accept it, and by way of irrevocability at once burnt his ships behind him—in devouring part of his dinner.

Thus fortified in his outlawry, he began to look about him. He was on a thickly wooded terrace with a blank wall of "outcrop" on one side nearly as high as the pines which pressed close against it. He had never seen it before; it was two or three miles from the highroad and seemed to be a virgin wilderness. But on close examination he could see, with the eye of a boy bred in a mining district, that the wall of outcrop had not escaped the attention of the mining prospector. There were marks of his pick in some attractive quartz seams of the wall, and farther on, a more ambitious attempt, evidently by a party of miners, to begin a tunnel, shown in an abandoned excavation and the heap of debris before it. It had evidently been abandoned for some time, as ferns already forced their green fronds through the stones and gravel, and the yerba buena vine was beginning to mat the surface of the heap. But the boy's fancy was quickly taken by the traces of a singular accident, and one which had perhaps arrested the progress of the excavators. The roots of a large pine-tree growing close to the wall had been evidently loosened by the excavators, and the tree had fallen, with one of its largest roots still in the opening the miners had made, and apparently blocking the entrance. The large tree lay, as it fell—midway across another but much smaller outcrop of rock which stood sharply about fifteen feet above the level of the terrace—with its gaunt, dead limbs in the air at a low angle. To Johnny's boyish fancy it seemed so easily balanced on the rock that but for its imprisoned root it would have made a capital see-saw. This he felt must be looked to hereafter. But here his attention was arrested by something more alarming. His quick ear, attuned like an animal's to all woodland sounds, detected the crackling of underwood in the

Bret Harte

distance. His equally sharp eye saw the figures of two men approaching. But as he recognized the features of one of them he drew back with a beating heart, a hushed breath, and hurriedly hid himself in the shadow. For he had seen that figure once before—flying before the sheriff and an armed posse—and had never forgotten it! It was the figure of Spanish Pete, a notorious desperado and sluice robber!

Finding he had been unobserved, the boy took courage, and his small faculties became actively alive. The two men came on together cautiously, and at a little distance the second man, whom Johnny did not know, parted from his companion and began to loiter up and down, looking around as if acting as a sentinel for the desperado, who advanced directly to the fallen tree. Suddenly the sentinel uttered an exclamation, and Spanish Pete paused. The sentinel was examining the ground near the heap of debris.

"What's up?" growled the desperado.

"Foot tracks! Weren't here before. And fresh ones, too."

Johnny's heart sank. It was where he had just passed.

Spanish Pete hurriedly joined his companion.

"Foot tracks be—!" he said scornfully. "What fool would be crawlin' round here barefooted? It's a young b'ar!"

Johnny knew the footprints were his own. Yet he recognized the truth of the resemblance; it was uncomplimentary, but he felt relieved. The desperado came forward, and to the boy's surprise began to climb the small ridge of outcrop until he reached the fallen tree. Johnny saw that he was carrying a heavy stone. "What's the blamed fool goin' to do?" he said to himself; the man's evident ignorance regarding footprints had lessened the boy's awe of him. But the stranger's next essay took Johnny's breath away. Standing on the fallen tree trunk at its axis on the outcrop, he began to rock it gently. To Johnny's surprise it began to move. The upper end descended slowly, lifting the root in the excavation at the lower end, and with it a mass of rock, and revealing a cavern behind large enough to admit a man. Johnny gasped. The desperado coolly deposited the heavy stone on the tree beyond its axis on the rock, so that it would keep the tree in position, leaped from the tree to the rock, and quickly descended, at which he was joined by the other man, who was carrying two heavy chamois-leather bags. They both proceeded to the opening thus miraculously disclosed, and disappeared in it.

Johnny sat breathless, wondering, expectant, but not daring to move. The men might come out at any moment; he had seen enough to know that their enterprise as well as their cave was a secret, and that the desperado would subject any witness to it, however innocent or unwilling, to horrible penalties. The time crept slowly by,—he heard every rap of a woodpecker in a distant tree; a blue jay dipped and lighted on a branch within his reach, but he dared not extend his hand; his legs were infested by ants; he even fancied he heard the dry, hollow rattle of a rattlesnake not a yard from him. And then the entrance of the cave was darkened, and the two men reappeared. Johnny stared. He would have rubbed his eyes if he had dared. They were not the same men! Did the cave contain others who had been all the while shut up in its dark recesses? Was there a band? Would they all swarm out upon him? Should he run for his life?

But the illusion was only momentary. A longer look at them convinced him that they were the same men in new clothes and disguised, and as one remounted the outcrop Johnny's keen eyes recognized him as Spanish Pete. He merely kicked away the stone; the root again descended gently over the opening, and the tree recovered its former angle. The two hurried away, but Johnny noticed that they were empty-handed. The bags had been left behind.

The boy waited patiently, listening with his ear to the ground, like an Indian, for the last rustle of fern and crackle of underbrush, and then emerged, stiff and cramped from his concealment. But he no longer thought of flight; curiosity and ambition burned in his small veins. He quickly climbed up the outcrop, picked up the fallen stone, and in spite of its weight lifted it to the prostrate tree. Here he paused, and from his coign of vantage looked and listened. The solitude was profound. Then mounting the tree and standing over its axis he tried to rock it as the others had. Alas! Johnny's heart was stout, his courage unlimited, his perception all-embracing, his ambition boundless; but his actual avoir-dupois was only that of a boy of ten. The tree did not move. But Johnny had played see-saw before, and quietly moved towards its highest part. It slowly descended under the changed centre of gravity, and the root arose, disclosing the opening as before. Yet here the little hero paused. He waited with his eyes fixed on the opening, ready to fly on the sallying out of any one who had remained concealed. He then placed the stone where he had stood, leaped down, and ran to the opening.

The change from the dazzling sunlight to the darkness confused him at first, and he could see nothing. On entering he stumbled over something which proved to be a bottle in which a candle was fitted, and a box of matches evidently used by the two men. Lighting the candle he could now discern that the cavern was only a few yards long, the beginning of a tunnel which the accident to the tree had stopped. In one corner lay the clothes that the men had left, and which for a moment seemed all that the cavern contained, but on removing them Johnny saw that they were thrown over a rifle, a revolver, and the two chamois-leather bags that the men had brought there. They were so heavy that the boy could scarcely lift them. His face flushed; his hands trembled with excitement. To a boy whose truant wanderings had given him a fair knowledge of mining, he knew that weight could have but one meaning! Gold! He hurriedly untied the nearest bag. But it was not the gold of the locality, of the tunnel, of the "bed rock"! It was "flake gold," the gold of the river! It had been taken from the miners' sluices in the distant streams. The bags before him were the spoils of the sluice robber,—spoils that could not be sold or even shown in the district without danger, spoils kept until they could be taken to Marysville or Sacramento for disposal. All this might have occurred to the mind of any boy of the locality who had heard the common gossip of his elders, but to Johnny's fancy an idea was kindled peculiarly his own! Here was a cavern like that of the "Forty Thieves" in the story book, and he was the "Ali Baba" who knew its secret! He was not obliged to say "Open Sesame," but he could say it if he liked, if he was showing it off to anybody!

Yet alas he also knew it was a secret he must keep to himself. He had nobody to trust it to. His father was a charcoal-burner of small means; a widower with two children, Johnny and his elder brother Sam. The latter, a flagrant incorrigible of twenty-two, with a tendency to dissipation and low company, had lately abandoned his father's roof, only to reappear at intervals of hilarious or maudlin intoxication. He had always been held up to Johnny as a warning, or with the gloomy prognosis that he, Johnny, was already following in his tortuous footsteps. Even if he were here he was not to be thought of as a confidant. Still less could he trust his father, who would be sure to bungle the secret with sheriffs and constables, and end by bringing down the vengeance of the gang upon the family. As for himself, he could not dispose of the gold if he were to take it.

The exhibition of a single flake of it to the adult public would arouse suspicion, and as it was Johnny's hard fate to be always doubted, he might be connected with the gang. As a truant he knew he had no moral standing, but he also had the superstition—quite characteristic of childhood—that being in possession of a secret he was a participant in its criminality—and bound, as it were, by terrible oaths! And then a new idea seized him. He carefully put back everything as he had found it, extinguished the candle, left the cave, remounted the tree, and closed the opening again as he had seen the others do it, with the addition of murmuring "Shut Sesame" to himself, and then ran away as fast as his short legs could carry him.

Well clear of the dangerous vicinity, he proceeded more leisurely for about a mile, until he came to a low whitewashed fence, inclosing a small cultivated patch and a neat farmhouse beyond. Here he paused, and, cowering behind the fence, with extraordinary facial contortions produced a cry not unlike the scream of a blue jay. Repeating it at intervals, he was presently relieved by observing the approach of a nankeen sunbonnet within the inclosure above the line of fence. Stopping before him, the sun-bonnet revealed a rosy little face, more than usually plump on one side, and a neck enormously wrapped in a scarf. It was "Meely" (Amelia) Stryker, a schoolmate, detained at home by "mumps," as Johnny was previously aware. For, with the famous indiscretion of some other great heroes, he was about to intrust his secret and his destiny to one of the weaker sex. And what were the minor possibilities of contagion to this?

"Playin' hookey ag'in?" said the young lady, with a cordial and even expansive smile, exclusively confined to one side of her face.

"Um! So'd you be ef you'd bin whar I hev," he said with

harrowing mystery.

"No!—say!" said Meely eagerly.

At which Johnny, clutching at the top of the fence, with hurried breath told his story. But not all. With the instinct of a true artist he withheld the manner in which the opening of the cave was revealed, said nothing about the tree, and, I grieve to say, added the words "Open Sesame" as the important factor to the operation. Neither did he mention the name of Spanish Pete. For all of which he was afterwards duly grateful.

"Meet me at the burnt pine down the crossroads at four o'clock," he said in conclusion, "and I'll show ye."

"Why not now?" said Meely impatiently.

"Couldn't. Much as my life is worth! Must keep watching out! You come at four."

And with an assuring nod he released the fence and trotted off. He returned cautiously in the direction of the cave; he was by no means sure that the robbers might not return that day, and his mysterious rendezvous with Meely veiled a certain prudence. And it was well! For as he stealthily crept around the face of the outcrop, hidden in the ferns, he saw from the altered angle of the tree that the cavern was opened. He remained motionless, with bated breath. Then he heard the sound of subdued voices from the cavern, and a figure emerged from the opening. Johnny grasped the ferns rigidly to check the dreadful cry that rose to his lips at its sight. For that figure was his own brother!

There was no mistaking that weak, wicked face, even then flushed with liquor! Johnny had seen it too often thus. But never before as a thief's face! He gave a little gasp, and fell back upon that strange reserve of apathy and reticence in which children are apt to hide their emotions from us at such a moment. He watched impassively the two other men who followed his brother out to give him a small bag and some instructions, and then returned within their cave, while his brother walked quickly away. He watched him disappear; he did not move, for even if he had followed him he could not bear to face him in his shame. And then out of his sullen despair came a boyish idea of revenge. It was those two men who had made his brother a thief!

He was very near the tree. He crept stealthily on his hands and knees through the bracken, and as stealthily climbed the wedge of outcrop, and then leaped like a wild cat on the tree. With incredible activity he lifted the balancing stone, and as the tree began to move, in a flash of perception transferred it to the other side of its axis, and felt the roots and debris, under that additional weight, descend quickly with something like a crash over the opening. Then he took to his heels. He ran so swiftly that all unknowingly he overtook a figure, who, turning, glanced at him, and then disappeared in the wood. It was his second and last view of his brother, as he never saw him again!

But now, strange to say, the crucial and most despairing moment of his day's experience had come. He had to face Meely Stryker under the burnt pine, and the promise he could not keep, and to tell her that he had lied to her. It was the only way to save his brother now! His small wits, and alas! his smaller methods, were equal to the despairing task. As soon as he saw her waiting under the tree he fell to capering and dancing with an extravagance in which hysteria had no small part. "Sold! sold! sold again, and got the money!" he laughed shrilly.

The girl looked at him with astonishment, which changed gradually to scorn, and then to anger. Johnny's heart sank, but he redoubled his antics.

"Who's sold?" she said disdainfully.

"You be. You swallered all that stuff about Ali Baba! You wanted to be Morgy Anna! Ho! ho! And I've made you play hookey—from home!"

"You hateful, horrid, little liar!"

Johnny accepted his punishment meekly—in his heart gratefully. "I reckoned you'd laugh and not get mad," he said submissively. The girl turned, with tears of rage and vexation in her eyes, and walked away. Johnny followed at a humble distance. Perhaps there was something instinctively touching in the boy's remorse, for they made it up before they reached her fence.

Nevertheless Johnny went home miserable. Luckily for him, his father was absent at a Vigilance Committee called to take cognizance of the late sluice robberies, and although this temporarily concealed his offense of truancy, the news of the vigilance meeting determined him to keep his lips sealed. He lay all night wondering how long it would take the robbers to dig themselves out of the cave, and whether they suspected their imprisonment was the work of an enemy or only an accident. For several days he avoided the locality, and even feared the vengeful appearance of Spanish Pete some night at his father's house. It was not until the end of a fortnight that he had the courage to revisit the spot. The tree was in its normal position, but immovable, and a great quantity of fresh debris at the mouth of the cave convinced him that the robbers, after escaping, had abandoned it as unsafe. His brother did not return, and either the activity of the Vigilance

Committee or the lack of a new place of rendezvous seemed to have dispersed the robbers from the locality, for they were not heard of again.

The next ten years brought an improvement to Mr. Starleigh's fortunes. Johnny Starleigh, then a student at San Jose, one morning found a newspaper clipping in a letter from Miss Amelia Stryker. It read as follows: "The excavators in the new tunnel in Heavystone Ridge lately discovered the skeletons of two unknown men, who had evidently been crushed and entombed some years previously, by the falling of a large tree over the mouth of their temporary refuge. From some river gold found with them, they were supposed to be part of the gang of sluice robbers who infested the locality some years ago, and were hiding from the Vigilants."

For a few days thereafter Johnny Starleigh was thoughtful and reserved, but he did not refer to the paragraph in answering the letter. He decided to keep it for later confidences, when Miss Stryker should become Mrs. Starleigh.

MISS PEGGY'S PROTEGES

The string of Peggy's sunbonnet had become untied—so had her right shoe. These were not unusual accidents to a country girl of ten, but as both of her hands were full she felt obliged to put down what she was carrying. This was further complicated by the nature of her burden—a half-fledged shrike and a baby gopher—picked up in her walk. It was impossible to wrap them both in her apron without serious peril to one or the other; she could not put either down without the chance of its escaping. "It's like that dreadful riddle of the ferryman who had to take the wolf and the sheep in his boat," said Peggy to herself, "though I don't believe anybody was ever so silly as to want to take a wolf across the river." But, looking up, she beheld the approach of Sam Bedell, a six-foot tunnelman of the "Blue Cement Lead," and, hailing him, begged him to hold one of her captives. The giant, loathing the little mouse-like ball of fur, chose the shrike. "Hold him by the feet, for he bites AWFUL," said Peggy, as the bird regarded Sam with the diabolically intense frown of his species. Then, dropping the gopher unconcernedly in her pocket, she proceeded to rearrange her toilet. The tunnelman waited patiently until Peggy had secured the nankeen sunbonnet around her fresh but freckled cheeks, and, with a reckless display of yellow flannel petticoat and stockings like peppermint sticks, had double-knotted her shoestrings viciously when he ventured

Bret Harte

to speak.

"Same old game, Peggy? Thought you'd got rather discouraged with your 'happy family,' arter that new owl o' yours had gathered 'em in."

Peggy's cheek flushed slightly at this ungracious allusion to a former collection of hers, which had totally disappeared one evening after the introduction of a new member in the shape of a singularly venerable and peaceful-looking horned owl.

"I could have tamed HIM, too," said Peggy indignantly, "if Ned Myers, who gave him to me, hadn't been training him to ketch things, and never let on anything about it to me. He was a reg'lar game owl!"

"And wot are ye goin' to do with the Colonel here?" said Sam, indicating under that gallant title the infant shrike, who, with his claws deeply imbedded in Sam's finger, was squatting like a malignant hunchback, and resisting his transfer to Peggy. "Won't HE make it rather lively for the others? He looks pow'ful discontented for one so young."

"That's his nater," said Peggy promptly. "Jess wait till I tame him. Ef he'd been left along o' his folks, he'd grow up like 'em. He's a 'butcher bird'—wot they call a 'nine-killer '—kills nine birds a day! Yes! True ez you live! Sticks 'em up on thorns outside his nest, jest like a butcher's shop, till he gets hungry. I've seen 'em!"

"And how do you kalkilate to tame him?" asked Sam.

"By being good to him and lovin' him," said Peggy, stroking the head of the bird with infinite gentleness.

"That means YOU'VE got to do all the butchering for him?"

said the cynical Sam.

Peggy shook her head, disdaining a verbal reply.

"Ye can't bring him up on sugar and crackers, like a Polly," persisted Sam.

"Ye ken do anythin' with critters, if you ain't afeerd of 'em and love 'em," said Peggy shyly.

The tall tunnelman, looking down into the depths of Peggy's sunbonnet, saw something in the round blue eyes and grave little mouth that made him think so too. But here Peggy's serious little face took a shade of darker concern as her arm went down deeper into her pocket, and her eyes got rounder.

"It's—it's—BURRERED OUT!" she said breathlessly.

The giant leaped briskly to one side. "Hol' on," said Peggy abstractedly. With infinite gravity she followed, with her fingers, a seam of her skirt down to the hem, popped them quickly under it, and produced, with a sigh of relief, the missing gopher.

"You'll do," said Sam, in fearful admiration. "Mebbe you'll make suthin' out o' the Colonel too. But I never took stock in that there owl. He was too durned self-righteous for a decent bird. Now, run along afore anythin' else fetches loose ag'in. So long!"

He patted the top of her sunbonnet, gave a little pull to the short brown braid that hung behind her temptingly,—which no miner was ever known to resist,—and watched her flutter off with her spoils. He had done so many times before, for the great, foolish heart of the Blue Cement Ridge had gone out to Peggy Baker, the little daughter of the blacksmith, quite early. There were others of the family, notably two elder sisters, invincible at picnics and dances, but Peggy was as necessary to these men as the blue jay that swung before them in the dim woods, the squirrel that whisked across their morning path, or the woodpecker who beat his tattoo at their midday meal from the hollow pine above them. She was part of the nature that kept them young. Her truancies and vagrancies concerned them not: she was a law to herself, like the birds and squirrels. There were bearded lips to hail her wherever she went, and a blue or red-shirted arm always stretched out in any perilous pass or dangerous crossing.

Her peculiar tastes were an outcome of her nature, assisted by her surroundings. Left a good deal to herself in her infancy, she made playfellows of animated nature around her, without much reference to selection or fitness, but always with a fearlessness that was the result of her own observation, and unhampered by tradition or other children's timidity. She had no superstition regarding the venom of toads, the poison of spiders, or the ear-penetrating capacity of earwigs. She had experiences and revelations of her own,—which she kept sacredly to herself, as children do,—and one was in regard to a rattlesnake, partly induced, however, by the indiscreet warning of her elders. She was cautioned NOT to take her bread and milk into the woods, and was told the affecting story of the little girl who was once regularly visited by a snake that partook of HER bread and milk, and who was ultimately found rapping the head of the snake for gorging more than his share, and not "taking a 'poon as me do." It is needless to say that this incautious caution fired Peggy's adventurous spirit. SHE took a bowlful of milk to the haunt of a "rattler" near her home, but, without making the pretense of sharing it, generously left the whole to the reptile. After repeating this hospitality for three or four days, she was amazed one morning on returning to the house to find the snake—an elderly one with a dozen rattles—

devotedly following her. Alarmed, not for her own safety nor that of her family, but for the existence of her grateful friend in danger of the blacksmith's hammer, she took a circuitous route leading it away. Then recalling a bit of woodland lore once communicated to her by a charcoal-burner, she broke a spray of the white ash, and laid it before her in the track of the rattlesnake. He stopped instantly, and remained motionless without crossing the slight barrier. She repeated this experiment on later occasions, until the reptile understood her. She kept the experience to herself, but one day it was witnessed by a tunnelman. On that day Peggy's reputation was made!

From this time henceforth the major part of Blue Cement Ridge became serious collectors for what was known as "Peggy's menagerie," and two of the tunnelmen constructed a stockaded inclosure—not half a mile from the blacksmith's cabin, but unknown to him—for the reception of specimens. For a long time its existence was kept a secret between Peggy and her loyal friends. Her parents, aware of her eccentric tastes only through the introduction of such smaller creatures as lizards, toads, and tarantulas into their house,— which usually escaped from their tin cans and boxes and sought refuge in the family slippers,—had frowned upon her zoological studies. Her mother found that her woodland rambles entailed an extraordinary wear and tear of her clothing. A pinafore reduced to ribbons by a young fox, and a straw hat half swallowed by a mountain kid, did not seem to be a natural incident to an ordinary walk to the schoolhouse. Her sisters thought her tastes "low," and her familiar association with the miners inconsistent with their own dignity. But Peggy went regularly to school, was a fair scholar in elementary studies (what she knew of natural history, in fact, quite startled her teachers), and being also a teachable child, was allowed some latitude. As for Peggy herself, she kept her own faith unshaken; her little creed, whose shibboleth was not "to be afraid" of God's creatures, but to "love 'em," sustained her through reprimand, torn clothing, and, it is to be feared, occasional bites and scratches from the loved ones themselves.

The unsuspected contiguity of the "menagerie" to the house had its drawbacks, and once nearly exposed her. A mountain wolf cub, brought especially for her from the higher northern Sierras with great trouble and expense by Jack Ryder, of the Lone Star Lead, unfortunately escaped from the menagerie just as the child seemed to be in a fair way of taming it. Yet it had been already familiarized enough with civilization to induce it to stop in its flight and curiously examine the blacksmith's shop. A shout from the blacksmith and a hurled hammer sent it flying again, with Mr. Baker and his assistant in full pursuit. But it quickly distanced them with its long, tireless gallop, and they were obliged to return to the forge, lost in wonder and conjecture. For the blacksmith had recognized it as a stranger to the locality, and as a man of oracular pretension had a startling theory to account for its presence. This he confided to the editor of the local paper, and the next issue contained an editorial paragraph: "Our presage of a severe winter in the higher Sierras, and consequent spring floods in the valleys, has been startlingly confirmed! Mountain wolves have been seen in Blue Cement Ridge, and our esteemed fellow citizen, Mr. Ephraim Baker, yesterday encountered a half-starved cub entering his premises in search of food. Mr. Baker is of the opinion that the mother of the cub, driven down by stress of weather, was in the immediate vicinity." Nothing but the distress of the only responsible mother of the cub, Peggy, and loyalty to her, kept Jack Ryder from exposing the absurdity publicly, but for weeks the camp fires of Blue Cement Ridge shook with the suppressed and unhallowed joy of the miners, who were in the guilty secret.

But, fortunately for Peggy, the most favored of her cherished possessions was not obliged to be kept secret. That one exception was an Indian dog! This was also a gift, and had been procured with great "difficulty" by a "packer" from an Indian encampment on the Oregon frontier. The "difficulty" was, in plain English, that it had been stolen from the Indians at some peril to the stealer's scalp. It was a mongrel to all appearances, of no recognized breed or outward significance, yet of a quality distinctly its own. It was absolutely and totally uncivilized. Whether this was a hereditary trait, or the result of degeneracy, no one knew. It refused to enter a house; it would not stay in a kennel. It would not eat in public, but gorged ravenously and stealthily in the shadows. It had the slink of a tramp, and in its patched and mottled hide seemed to simulate the rags of a beggar. It had the tirelessness without the affected limp of a coyote. Yet it had none of the ferocity of barbarians. With teeth that could gnaw through the stoutest rope and toughest lariat, it never bared them in anger. It was cringing without being amiable or submissive; it was gentle without being affectionate.

Yet almost insensibly it began to yield to Peggy's faith and kindness. Gradually it seemed to single her out as the one being in this vast white-faced and fully clothed community that it could trust. It presently allowed her to half drag, half lead it to and fro from school, although on the approach of a stranger it would bite through the rope or frantically endeavor to efface itself in Peggy's petticoats. It was trying, even to the child's sweet gravity, to face the ridicule excited by its appearance on the road; and its habit of carrying its tail between its legs—at such an inflexible curve that, on the authority of Sam Bedell, a misstep caused it to "turn a back somersault"—was painfully disconcerting. But Peggy endured this, as she did the greater dangers of the High Street in the settlement, where she had often, at her own risk, absolutely to drag the dazed and bewildered creature from under the wheels of carts and the heels of horses. But this shyness wore off—or rather was eventually lost in the dog's complete and utter absorption in Peggy. His limited intelligence and imperfect perceptions were excited for her alone. His singularly keen scent detected her wherever or how remote she might be. Her passage along a "blind trail," her deviations from the school path, her more distant excursions, were all mysteriously known to him. It seemed as if his senses were concentrated in this one faculty. No matter how unexpected or unfamiliar the itinerary, "Lo, the poor Indian"—as the men had nicknamed him (in possible allusion to his "untutored mind")—always arrived promptly and silently.

It was to this singular faculty that Peggy owed one of her strangest experiences. One Saturday afternoon she was returning from an errand to the village when she was startled by the appearance of Lo in her path. For the reason already given, she no longer took him with her to these active haunts of civilization, but had taught him on such occasions to remain as a guard outside the stockade which contained her treasures. After reading him a severe lecture on this flagrant abandonment of his trust, enforced with great seriousness and an admonitory forefinger, she was concerned to see that the animal appeared less agitated by her reproof than by some other disturbance. He ran ahead of her, instead of at her heels, as was his usual custom, and barked—a thing he rarely did. Presently she thought she discovered the cause of this in the appearance from the wood of a dozen men armed with guns. They seemed to be strangers, but among them she recognized the deputy sheriff of the settlement. The leader noticed her, and, after a word or two with the others, the deputy approached her.

"You and Lo had better be scooting home by the highroad, outer this—or ye might get hurt," he said, half playfully, half seriously.

Peggy looked fearlessly at the men and their guns.

"Look ez ef you was huntin'?" she said curiously.

"We are!" said the leader.

"Wot you huntin'?"

The deputy glanced at the others. "B'ar!" he replied.

"Ba'r!" repeated the child with the quick resentment which a palpable falsehood always provoked in her. "There ain't no b'ar in ten miles! See yourself huntin' b'ar! Ho!"

The man laughed. "Never you mind, missy," said the deputy, "you trot along!" He laid his hand very gently on her head, faced her sunbonnet towards the near highway, gave the usual parting pull to her brown pigtail, added, "Make a bee-line home," and turned away.

Lo uttered the first growl known in his history. Whereat Peggy said, with lofty forbearance, "Serve you jest right ef I set my dog on you."

But force is no argument, and Peggy felt this truth even of herself and Lo. So she trotted away. Nevertheless, Lo showed signs of hesitation. After a few moments Peggy herself hesitated and looked back. The men had spread out under the trees, and were already lost in the woods. But there was more than one trail through it, and Peggy knew it.

And here an alarming occurrence startled her. A curiously striped brown and white squirrel whisked past her and ran up a tree. Peggy's round eyes became rounder. There was but one squirrel of that kind in all the length and breadth of Blue Cement Ridge, and that was in the menagerie! Even as she looked it vanished. Peggy faced about and ran back to the road in the direction of the stockade, Lo bounding before her. But another surprise awaited her. There was the clutter of short wings under the branches, and the sunlight flashed upon the iris throat of a wood-duck as it swung out of sight past her. But in this single glance Peggy recognized one of the latest and most precious of her acquisitions. There was no mistake now! With a despairing little cry to Lo, "The menagerie's broke loose!" she ran like the wind towards it. She cared no longer for the mandate of the men; the trail she had taken was out of their sight; they were proceeding so slowly and cautiously that she and Lo quickly distanced them in the same direction. She would have yet time to reach the stockade and secure what was left of her treasures before they came up and drove her away. Yet she had to make a long circuit to avoid the blacksmith's shop and cabin, before she saw the stockade, lifting its four-foot walls around an inclosure a dozen feet square, in the midst of a manzanita thicket. But she could see also broken coops, pens, cages, and boxes lying before it, and stopped once, even in her grief and indignation, to pick up a ruby-throated lizard, one of its late inmates that had stopped in the trail, stiffened to stone at her approach. The next moment she was before the roofless walls, and then stopped, stiffened like the lizard. For out of that peaceful ruin which had once held the wild and untamed vagabonds of earth and sky, arose a type of savagery and barbarism the child had never before looked upon,—the head and shoulders of a hunted, desperate man!

His head was bare, and his hair matted with sweat over his forehead; his face was unshorn, and the black roots of his beard showed against the deadly pallor of his skin, except where it was scratched by thorns, or where the red spots over his cheek bones made his cheeks look as if painted. His eyes were as insanely bright, he panted as quickly, he showed his white teeth as perpetually, his movements were as convulsive, as those captured animals she had known. Yet he did not attempt to fly, and it was only when, with a sudden effort and groan of pain, he half lifted himself above the stockade, that she saw that his leg, bandaged with his cravat and handkerchief, stained a dull red, dragged helplessly beneath him. He stared at her vacantly for a moment, and then looked hurriedly into the wood behind her.

The child was more interested than frightened, and more curious than either. She had grasped the situation at a glance. It was the hunted and the hunters. Suddenly he started and reached for his rifle, which he had apparently set down outside when he climbed into the stockade. He had just caught sight of a figure emerging from the wood at a distance. But the weapon was out of his reach.

"Hand me that gun!" he said roughly.

But Peggy did not stir. The figure came more plainly and quite unconsciously into full view, an easy shot at that distance.

The man uttered a horrible curse, and turned a threatening face on the child. But Peggy had seen something like that in animals SHE had captured. She only said gravely,—

"Ef you shoot that gun you'll bring 'em all down on you!"

"All?" he demanded.

"Yes! a dozen folks with guns like yours," said Peggy. "You jest crouch down and lie low. Don't move! Watch me."

The man dropped below the stockade. Peggy ran swiftly

towards the unsuspecting figure, evidently the leader of the party, but deviated slightly to snatch a tiny spray from a white-ash tree. She never knew that in that brief interval the wounded man, after a supreme effort, had possessed himself of his weapon, and for a moment had covered HER with its deadly muzzle. She ran on fearlessly until she saw that she had attracted the attention of the leader, when she stopped and began to wave the white-ash wand before her. The leader halted, conferred with some one behind him, who proved to be the deputy sheriff. Stepping out he advanced towards Peggy, and called sharply,

"I told you to get out of this! Come, be quick!"

"You'd better get out yourself," said Peggy, waving her ash spray, "and quicker, too."

The deputy stopped, staring at the spray. "Wot's up?"

"Rattlers."

"Where?"

"Everywhere round ye—a reg'lar nest of 'em! That's your way round!" She pointed to the right, and again began beating the underbrush with her wand. The men had, meantime, huddled together in consultation. It was evident that the story of Peggy and her influence on rattlesnakes was well known, and, in all probability, exaggerated. After a pause, the whole party filed off to the right, making a long circuit of the unseen stockade, and were presently lost in the distance. Peggy ran back to the fugitive. The fire of savagery and desperation in his eyes had gone out, but had been succeeded by a glazing film of faintness.

"Can you—get me—some water?" he whispered.

The stockade was near a spring,—a necessity for the menagerie. Peggy brought him water in a dipper. She sighed a little; her "butcher bird"—now lost forever—had been the last to drink from it!

The water seemed to revive him. "The rattlesnakes scared the cowards," he said, with an attempt to smile. "Were there many rattlers?"

"There wasn't ANY," said Peggy, a little spitefully, "'cept YOU—a two-legged rattler!"

The rascal grinned at the compliment.

"ONE-legged, you mean," he said, indicating his helpless limb.

Peggy's heart relented slightly. "Wot you goin' to do now?" she said. "You can't stay on THERE, you know. It b'longs to ME!" She was generous, but practical.

"Were those things I fired out yours?"

"Yes."

"Mighty rough of me."

Peggy was slightly softened. "Kin you walk?"

"No."

"Kin you crawl?"

"Not as far as a rattler."

"Ez far ez that clearin'?"

"Yes."

"There's a hoss tethered out in that clearin'. I kin shift him to this end."

"You're white all through," said the man gravely.

Peggy ran off to the clearing. The horse belonged to Sam Bedell, but he had given Peggy permission to ride it whenever she wished. This was equivalent, in Peggy's mind, to a permission to PLACE him where she wished. She consequently led him to a point nearest the stockade, and, thoughtfully, close beside a stump. But this took some time, and when she arrived she found the fugitive already there, very thin and weak, but still smiling.

"Ye kin turn him loose when you get through with him; he'll find his way back," said Peggy. "Now I must go."

Without again looking at the man, she ran back to the stockade. Then she paused until she heard the sound of hoofs crossing the highway in the opposite direction from which the pursuers had crossed, and knew that the fugitive had got away. Then she took the astonished and still motionless lizard from her pocket, and proceeded to restore the broken coops and cages to the empty stockade.

But she never reconstructed her menagerie nor renewed her collection. People said she had tired of her whim, and that really she was getting too old for such things. Perhaps she was. But she never got old enough to reveal her story of the last wild animal she had tamed by kindness. Nor was she quite sure of it herself, until a few years afterwards on Commencement Day at a boarding-school at San Jose, when they pointed out to her one of the most respectable trustees. But they said he was once a gambler, who had shot a man with whom he had quarreled, and was nearly caught and lynched by a Vigilance Committee.

Bret Harte

THE GODDESS OF EXCELSIOR

When the two isolated mining companies encamped on Sycamore Creek discovered on the same day the great "Excelsior Lead," they met around a neutral camp fire with that grave and almost troubled demeanor which distinguished the successful prospector in those days. Perhaps the term "prospectors" could hardly be used for men who had labored patiently and light-heartedly in the one spot for over three years to gain a daily yield from the soil which gave them barely the necessaries of life. Perhaps this was why, now that their reward was beyond their most sanguine hopes, they mingled with this characteristic gravity an ambition and resolve peculiarly their own. Unlike most successful miners, they had no idea of simply realizing their wealth and departing to invest or spend it elsewhere, as was the common custom. On the contrary, that night they formed a high resolve to stand or fall by their claims, to develop the resources of the locality, to build up a town, and to devote themselves to its growth and welfare. And to this purpose they bound themselves that night by a solemn and legal compact.

Many circumstances lent themselves to so original a determination. The locality was healthful, picturesque, and fertile. Sycamore Creek, a considerable tributary of the Sacramento, furnished them a generous water supply at all seasons; its banks were well wooded and interspersed with undulating meadow land. Its distance from stage-coach communication—nine miles—could easily be abridged by a wagon road over a practically level country. Indeed, all the conditions for a thriving settlement were already there. It was natural, therefore, that the most sanguine anticipations were indulged by the more youthful of the twenty members of this sacred compact. The sites of a hotel, a bank, the express company's office, stage office, and court-house, with other necessary buildings, were all mapped out and supplemented by a theatre, a public park, and a terrace along the river bank! It was only when Clinton Grey, an intelligent but youthful member, on offering a plan of the town with five avenues eighty feet wide, radiating from a central plaza and the court-house, explained that "it could be commanded by artillery in case of an armed attack upon the building," that it was felt that a line must be drawn in anticipatory suggestion. Nevertheless, although their determination was unabated, at the end of six months little had been done beyond the building of a wagon road and the importation of new machinery for the working of the lead. The peculiarity of their design debarred any tentative or temporary efforts; they wished the whole settlement to spring up in equal perfection, so that the first stage-coach over the new road could arrive upon the completed town. "We don't want to show up in a 'b'iled shirt' and a plug hat, and our trousers stuck in our boots," said a figurative speaker. Nevertheless, practical necessity compelled them to build the hotel first for their own occupation, pending the erection of their private dwellings on allotted sites. The hotel, a really elaborate structure for the locality and period, was a marvel to the workmen and casual teamsters. It was luxuriously fitted and furnished. Yet it was in connection with this outlay that the event occurred which had a singular effect upon the fancy of the members.

Washington Trigg, a Western member, who had brought up the architect and builder from San Francisco, had returned in a state of excitement. He had seen at an art exhibition in that city a small replica of a famous statue of California, and, without consulting his fellow members, had ordered a larger copy for the new settlement. He, however, made up for his precipitancy by an extravagant description of his purchase, which impressed even the most cautious. "It's the figger of a mighty pretty girl, in them spirit clothes they allus wear, holding a divinin' rod for findin' gold afore her in one hand; all the while she's hidin' behind her, in the other hand, a branch o' thorns out of sight. The idea bein'—don't you see?—that blamed old 'forty-niners like us, or ordinary greenhorns, ain't allowed to see the difficulties they've got to go through before reaching a strike. Mighty cute, ain't it? It's to be made life-size,—that is, about the size of a girl of that kind, don't you see?" he explained somewhat vaguely, "and will look powerful fetchin' standin' onto a pedestal in the hall of the hotel." In reply to some further cautious inquiry as to the exact details of the raiment and of any possible shock to the modesty of lady guests at the hotel, he replied confidently, "Oh, THAT'S all right! It's the regulation uniform of goddesses and angels,—sorter as if they'd caught up a sheet or a cloud to fling round 'em before coming into this world afore folks; and being an allegory, so to speak, it ain't as if it was me or you prospectin' in high water. And, being of bronze, it"—

"Looks like a squaw, eh?" interrupted a critic, "or a cursed Chinaman?"

"And if it's of metal, it will weigh a ton! How are we going to get it up here?" said another.

But here Mr. Trigg was on sure ground. "I've ordered it cast holler, and, if necessary, in two sections," he returned triumphantly. "A child could tote it round and set it up."

Its arrival was therefore looked forward to with great expectancy when the hotel was finished and occupied by the combined Excelsior companies. It was to come from New York via San Francisco, where, however, there was some delay in its transshipment, and still further delay at Sacramento. It finally reached the settlement over the new wagon road, and was among the first freight carried there by the new express company, and delivered into the new express office. The box—a packing-case, nearly three feet square by five feet long—bore superficial marks of travel and misdirection, inasmuch as the original address was quite obliterated and the outside lid covered with corrected labels. It was carried to a private sitting-room in the hotel, where its beauty was to be first disclosed to the president of the united companies, three of the committee, and the excited and triumphant purchaser. A less favored crowd of members and workmen gathered curiously outside the room. Then the lid was carefully removed, revealing a quantity of shavings and packing paper which still hid the outlines of the goddess. When this was promptly lifted a stare of blank astonishment fixed the faces of the party! It was succeeded by a quick, hysteric laugh, and then a dead silence.

Before them lay a dressmaker's dummy, the wire and padded model on which dresses are fitted and shown. With its armless and headless bust, abruptly ending in a hooped wire skirt, it completely filled the sides of the box.

"Shut the door," said the president promptly.

The order was obeyed. The single hysteric shriek of laughter had been followed by a deadly, ironical silence. The president, with supernatural gravity, lifted it out and set it up on its small, round, disk-like pedestal.

"It's some cussed fool blunder of that confounded express company," burst out the unlucky purchaser. But there was no echo to his outburst. He looked around with a timid, tentative smile. But no other smile followed his.

"It looks," said the president, with portentous gravity, "like the beginnings of a fine woman, that MIGHT show up, if you gave her time, into a first-class goddess. Of course she ain't all here; other boxes with sections of her, I reckon, are under way from her factory, and will meander along in the course of the year. Considerin' this as a sample—I think, gentlemen," he added, with gloomy precision, "we are prepared to accept it, and signify we'll take more."

"It ain't, perhaps, exactly the idee that we've been led to expect from previous description," said Dick Flint, with deeper seriousness; "for instance, this yer branch of thorns we heard of ez bein' held behind her is wantin', as is the arms that held it; but even if they had arrived, anybody could see the thorns through them wires, and so give the hull show away."

"Jam it into its box again, and we'll send it back to the confounded express company with a cussin' letter," again thundered the wretched purchaser.

"No, sonny," said the president with gentle but gloomy determination, "we'll fasten on to this little show jest as it is, and see what follows. It ain't every day that a first-class sell like this is worked off on us ACCIDENTALLY."

It was quite true! The settlement had long since exhausted every possible form of practical joking, and languished for a new sensation. And here it was! It was not a thing to be treated angrily, nor lightly, nor dismissed with that single hysteric laugh. It was capable of the greatest possibilities!

Indeed, as Washington Trigg looked around on the imperturbably ironical faces of his companions, he knew that they felt more true joy over the blunder than they would in the possession of the real statue. But an exclamation from the fifth member, who was examining the box, arrested their attention.

"There's suthin' else here!"

He had found under the heavier wrapping a layer of tissue-paper, and under that a further envelope of linen, lightly stitched together. A knife blade quickly separated the stitches, and the linen was carefully unfolded. It displayed a beautifully trimmed evening dress of pale blue satin, with a dressing-gown of some exquisite white fabric armed with lace. The men gazed at it in silence, and then the one single expression broke from their lips,—

"Her duds!"

"Stop, boys," said "Clint" Grey, as a movement was made to lift the dress towards the model, "leave that to a man who knows. What's the use of my having left five grown-up sisters in the States if I haven't brought a little experience away with me? This sort of thing ain't to be 'pulled on' like trousers. No, sir!—THIS is the way she's worked."

With considerable dexterity, unexpected gentleness, and some taste, he shook out the folds of the skirt delicately and lifted it over the dummy, settling it skillfully upon the wire hoops, and drawing the bodice over the padded shoulders. This he then proceeded to fasten with hooks and eyes,—a work of some patience. Forty eager fingers stretched out to assist him, but were waved aside, with a look of pained decorum as he gravely completed his task. Then falling back, he bade the others do the same, and they formed a contemplative semicircle before the figure.

Up to that moment a delighted but unsmiling consciousness of their own absurdities, a keen sense of the humorous possibilities of the original blunder, and a mischievous recognition of the mortification of Trigg—whose only safety now lay in accepting the mistake in the same spirit—had determined these grown-up schoolboys to artfully protract a joke that seemed to be providentially delivered into their hands. But NOW an odd change crept on them. The light from the open window that gave upon the enormous pines and the rolling prospect up to the dim heights of the Sierras fell upon this strange, incongruous, yet perfectly artistic figure. For the dress was the skillful creation of a great Parisian artist, and in its exquisite harmony of color, shape, and material it not only hid the absurd model, but clothed it with an alarming grace and refinement! A queer feeling of awe, of shame, and of unwilling admiration took possession of them. Some of them—from remote Western towns—had never seen the like before; those who HAD had forgotten it in those five years of self-exile, of healthy independence, and of contiguity to Nature in her unaffected simplicity. All had been familiar with the garish, extravagant, and dazzling femininity of the Californian towns and cities, but never had they known anything approaching the ideal grace of this type of exalted, even if artificial, womanhood. And although in the fierce freedom of their little republic they had laughed to scorn such artificiality, a few yards of satin and lace cunningly fashioned, and thrown over a frame of wood and wire, touched them now with a strange sense of its superiority. The better to show its attractions, Clinton Grey had placed the figure near a full-length, gold-framed mirror, beside a marble-topped table. Yet how cheap and tawdry these splendors showed beside this work of art! How cruel was the contrast of their own rough working clothes to this miracle of adornment which that same mirror reflected! And even when Clinton Grey, the enthusiast, looked towards his beloved woods for relief, he could not help thinking of them as a more fitting frame for this strange goddess than this new house into which she had strayed. Their gravity became real; their gibes in some strange way had vanished.

"Must have cost a pile of money," said one, merely to break an embarrassing silence.

"My sister had a friend who brought over a dress from Paris, not as high-toned as that, that cost five hundred dollars," said Clinton Grey.

"How much did you say that spirit-clad old rag of yours cost—thorns and all?" said the president, turning sharply on Trigg.

Trigg swallowed this depreciation of his own purchase meekly. "Seven hundred and fifty dollars, without the express charges."

"That's only two-fifty more," said the president thoughtfully, "if we call it quits."

"But," said Trigg in alarm, "we must send it back."

"Not much, sonny," said the president promptly. "We'll hang on to this until we hear where that thorny old chump of yours has fetched up and is actin' her conundrums, and mebbe we can swap even."

"But how will we explain it to the boys?" queried Trigg. "They're waitin' outside to see it."

"There WON'T be any explanation," said the president, in the same tone of voice in which he had ordered the door shut. "We'll just say that the statue hasn't come, which is the frozen truth; and this box only contained some silk curtain decorations we'd ordered, which is only half a lie. And," still more firmly, "THIS SECRET DOESN'T GO OUT OF THIS ROOM, GENTLEMEN—or I ain't your president! I'm not going to let you give yourselves away to that crowd outside—you hear me? Have you ever allowed your unfettered intellect to consider what they'd say about this,— what a godsend it would be to every man we'd ever had a 'pull' on in this camp? Why, it would last 'em a whole year; we'd never hear the end of it! No, gentlemen! I prefer to live here without shootin' my fellow man, but I can't promise it if they once start this joke agin us!"

There was a swift approval of this sentiment, and the five members shook hands solemnly.

"Now," said the president, "we'll just fold up that dress again, and put it with the figure in this closet"—he opened a large dressing-chest in the suite of rooms in which they stood— "and we'll each keep a key. We'll retain this room for committee purposes, so that no one need see the closet. See? Now take off the dress! Be careful there! You're not handlin' pay dirt, though it's about as expensive! Steady!"

Yet it was wonderful to see the solicitude and care with which the dress was re-covered and folded in its linen wrapper.

"Hold on," exclaimed Trigg,—as the dummy was lifted into the chest,—"we haven't tried on the other dress!"

"Yes! yes!" repeated the others eagerly; "there's another!"

"We'll keep that for next committee meeting, gentlemen," said the president decisively. "Lock her up, Trigg."

The three following months wrought a wonderful change in Excelsior,—wonderful even in that land of rapid growth and progress. Their organized and matured plans, executed by a full force of workmen from the county town, completed the twenty cottages for the members, the bank, and the town hall. Visitors and intending settlers flocked over the new wagon road to see this new Utopia, whose founders, holding the land and its improvements as a corporate company, exercised the right of dictating the terms on which settlers were admitted. The feminine invasion was not yet potent enough to affect their consideration, either through any refinement or attractiveness, being composed chiefly of the industrious wives and daughters of small traders or temporary artisans. Yet it was found necessary to confide the hotel to the management of Mr. Dexter Marsh, his wife, and one intelligent but somewhat plain daughter, who looked after the accounts. There were occasional lady visitors at the hotel, attracted from the neighboring towns and settlements by its picturesqueness and a vague suggestiveness of its being a watering-place—and there was the occasional flash in the decorous street of a Sacramento or San Francisco gown. It is needless to say that to the five men who held the guilty secret of Committee Room No. 4 it only strengthened their belief in the super-elegance of their hidden treasure. At their last meeting they had fitted the second dress—which turned out to be a vapory summer house-frock or morning wrapper—over the dummy, and opinions were divided as to its equality with the first. However, the same subtle harmony of detail and grace of proportion characterized it.

"And you see," said Clint Grey, "it's jest the sort o' rig in which a man would be most likely to know her—and not in her war-paint, which would be only now and then."

Already "SHE" had become an individuality!

"Hush!" said the president. He had turned towards the door, at which some one was knocking lightly.

"Come in."

The door opened upon Miss Marsh, secretary and hotel assistant. She had a business aspect, and an open letter in her hand, but hesitated at the evident confusion she had occasioned. Two of the gentlemen had absolutely blushed, and the others regarded her with inane smiles or affected seriousness. They all coughed slightly.

"I beg your pardon," she said, not ungracefully, a slight color coming into her sallow cheek, which, in conjunction with the gold eye-glasses, gave her, at least in the eyes of the impressible Clint, a certain piquancy. "But my father said you were here in committee and I might consult you. I can come again, if you are busy."

She had addressed the president, partly from his office, his comparatively extreme age—he must have been at least thirty!—and possibly for his extremer good looks. He said hurriedly, "It's just an informal meeting;" and then, more politely, "What can we do for you?"

"We have an application for a suite of rooms next week," she said, referring to the letter, "and as we shall be rather full, father thought you gentlemen might be willing to take another larger room for your meetings, and give up these, which are part of a suite—and perhaps not exactly suitable"—

"Quite impossible!" "Quite so!" "Really out of the question," said the members, in a rapid chorus.

The young girl was evidently taken aback at this unanimity of opposition. She stared at them curiously, and then glanced around the room. "We're quite comfortable here," said the president explanatorily, "and—in fact—it's just what we want."

"We could give you a closet like that which you could lock up, and a mirror," she suggested, with the faintest trace of a smile.

"Tell your father, Miss Marsh," said the president, with dignified politeness, "that while we cannot submit to any change, we fully appreciate his business foresight, and are quite prepared to see that the hotel is properly compensated for our retaining these rooms." As the young girl withdrew with a puzzled curtsy he closed the door, placed his back against it, and said,—

"What the deuce did she mean by speaking of that closet?"

"Reckon she allowed we kept some fancy drinks in there," said Trigg; "and calkilated that we wanted the marble stand and mirror to put our glasses on and make it look like a swell private bar, that's all!"

"Humph," said the president.

Their next meeting, however, was a hurried one, and as the president arrived late, when the door closed smartly behind him he was met by the worried faces of his colleagues.

"Here's a go!" said Trigg excitedly, producing a folded paper. "The game's up, the hull show is busted; that cussed old statue—the reg'lar old hag herself—is on her way here! There's a bill o' lading and the express company's letter, and she'll be trundled down here by express at any moment."

"Well?" said the president quietly.

"Well!" replied the members aghast. "Do you know what that means?"

"That we must rig her up in the hall on a pedestal, as we reckoned to do," returned the president coolly.

"But you don't sabe," said Clinton Grey; "that's all very well as to the hag, but now we must give HER up," with an adoring glance towards the closet.

"Does the letter say so?"

"No," said Trigg hesitatingly, "no! But I reckon we can't keep BOTH."

"Why not?" said the president imperturbably, "if we paid for 'em?"

As the men only stared in reply he condescended to explain.

"Look here! I calculated all these risks after our last meeting. While you boys were just fussin' round, doin' nothing, I wrote to the express company that a box of women's damaged duds had arrived here, while we were looking for our statue; that you chaps were so riled at bein' sold by them that you dumped the whole blamed thing in the creek. But I added, if they'd let me know what the damage was, I'd send 'em a draft to cover it. After a spell of waitin' they said they'd call it square for two hundred dollars, considering our disappointment. And I sent the draft. That's spurred them up to get over our statue, I reckon. And, now that it's coming, it will set us right with the boys."

"And SHE," said Clinton Grey again, pointing to the locked chest, "belongs to us?"

"Until we can find some lady guest that will take her with the rooms," returned the president, a little cynically.

But the arrival of the real statue and its erection in the hotel vestibule created a new sensation. The members of the Excelsior Company were loud in its praises except the executive committee, whose coolness was looked upon by the others as an affectation of superiority. It awakened the criticism and jealousy of the nearest town.

"We hear," said the "Red Dog Advertiser," "that the long-promised statue has been put up in that high-toned Hash Dispensary they call a hotel at Excelsior. It represents an emaciated squaw in a scanty blanket gathering roots, and carrying a bit of thorn-bush kindlings behind her. The high-toned, close corporation of Excelsior may consider this a fair allegory of California; WE should say it looks mighty like a prophetic forecast of a hard winter on Sycamore Creek and scarcity of provisions. However, it isn't our funeral, though it's rather depressing to the casual visitor on his way to dinner. For a long time this work of art was missing and supposed to be lost, but by being sternly and persistently rejected at every express office on the route, it was at last taken in at Excelsior."

There was some criticism nearer home.

"What do you think of it, Miss Marsh?" said the president politely to that active young secretary, as he stood before it in the hall. The young woman adjusted her eye-glasses over her aquiline nose.

"As an idea or a woman, sir?"

"As a woman, madam," said the president, letting his brown eyes slip for a moment from Miss Marsh's corn-colored crest over her straight but scant figure down to her smart slippers.

"Well, sir, she could wear YOUR boots, and there isn't a corset in Sacramento would go round her."

"Thank you!" he returned gravely, and moved away. For a moment a wild idea of securing possession of the figure some dark night, and, in company with his fellow-conspirators, of trying those beautiful clothes upon her, passed through his mind, but he dismissed it. And then occurred a strange incident, which startled even his cool, American sanity.

It was a beautiful moonlight night, and he was returning to a bedroom at the hotel which he temporarily occupied during the painting of his house. It was quite late, he having spent the evening with a San Francisco friend after a business conference which assured him of the remarkable prosperity of Excelsior. It was therefore with some human exaltation that he looked around the sleeping settlement which had sprung up under the magic wand of their good fortune. The full moon had idealized their youthful designs with something of their own youthful coloring, graciously softening the garish freshness of paint and plaster, hiding with discreet obscurity the disrupted banks and broken woods at the beginning and end of their broad avenues, paving the rough river terrace with tessellated shadows, and even touching the rapid stream which was the source of their wealth with a Pactolean glitter.

The windows of the hotel before him, darkened within, flashed in the moonbeams like the casements of Aladdin's palace. Mingled with his ambition, to-night, were some softer fancies, rarely indulged by him in his forecast of the future of Excelsior—a dream of some fair partner in his life, after this task was accomplished, yet always of some one moving in a larger world than his youth had known. Rousing the half sleeping porter, he found, however, only the spectral gold-seeker in the vestibule,—the rays of his solitary candle falling upon her divining-rod with a quaint persistency that seemed to point to the stairs he was ascending. When he reached the first landing the rising wind through an open window put out his light, but, although the staircase was in darkness, he could see the long corridor above illuminated by the moonlight throughout its whole length. He had nearly reached it when the slow but unmistakable rustle of a dress in the distance caught his ear. He paused, not only in the interest of delicacy, but with a sudden nervous thrill he could not account for. The rustle came nearer—he could hear the distinct frou-frou of satin; and then, to his bewildered eyes, what seemed to be the figure of the dummy, arrayed in the pale blue evening dress he knew so well, passed gracefully and majestically down the corridor. He could see the shapely folds of the skirt, the symmetry of the bodice, even the harmony of the trimmings. He raised his eyes, half affrightedly, prepared to see the headless shoulders, but they—and what seemed to be a head—were concealed in a floating "cloud" or nubia of some fleecy tissue, as if for protection from the evening air. He remained for an instant motionless, dazed by this apparent motion of an inanimate figure; but as the absurdity of the idea struck him he hurriedly but stealthily ascended the remaining stairs, resolved to follow it. But he was only in time to see it turn into the angle of another corridor, which, when he had reached it, was empty. The figure had vanished!

His first thought was to go to the committee room and examine the locked closet. But the key was in his desk at home, he had no light, and the room was on the other side of the house. Besides, he reflected that even the detection of the figure would involve the exposure of the very secret they had kept intact so long. He sought his bedroom, and went quietly

Bret Harte

to bed. But not to sleep; a curiosity more potent than any sense of the trespass done him kept him tossing half the night. Who was this woman whom the clothes fitted so well? He reviewed in his mind the guests in the house, but he knew none who could have carried off this masquerade so bravely.

In the morning early he made his way to the committee room, but as he approached was startled to observe two pairs of boots, a man's and a woman's, conjugally placed before its door. Now thoroughly indignant, he hurried to the office, and was confronted by the face of the fair secretary. She colored quickly on seeing him—but the reason was obvious.

"You are coming to scold me, sir! But it is not my fault. We were full yesterday afternoon when your friend from San Francisco came here with his wife. We told him those were YOUR rooms, but he said he would make it right with you— and my father thought you would not be displeased for once. Everything of yours was put into another room, and the closet remains locked as you left it."

Amazed and bewildered, the president could only mutter a vague apology and turn away. Had his friend's wife opened the door with another key in some fit of curiosity and disported herself in those clothes? If so, she DARE not speak of her discovery.

An introduction to the lady at breakfast dispelled this faint hope. She was a plump woman, whose generous proportions could hardly have been confined in that pale blue bodice; she was frank and communicative, with no suggestion of mischievous concealment.

Nevertheless, he made a firm resolution. As soon as his friends left he called a meeting of the committee. He briefly informed them of the accidental occupation of the room, but for certain reasons of his own said nothing of his ghostly experience. But he put it to them plainly that no more risks must be run, and that he should remove the dresses and dummy to his own house. To his considerable surprise this suggestion was received with grave approval and a certain strange relief.

"We kinder thought of suggesting it to you before," said Mr. Trigg slowly, "and that mebbe we've played this little game long enough—for suthin's happened that's makin' it anything but funny. We'd have told you before, but we dassent! Speak out, Clint, and tell the president what we saw the other night, and don't mince matters."

The president glanced quickly and warningly around him. "I thought," he said sternly, "that we'd dropped all fooling. It's no time for practical joking now!"

"Honest Injun—it's gospel truth! Speak up, Clint!"

The president looked on the serious faces around him, and was himself slightly awed.

"It's a matter of two or three nights ago," said Grey slowly, "that Trigg and I were passing through Sycamore Woods, just below the hotel. It was after twelve—bright moonlight, so that we could see everything as plain as day, and we were dead sober. Just as we passed under the sycamores Trigg grabs my arm, and says, 'Hi!' I looked up, and there, not ten yards away, standing dead in the moonlight, was that dummy! She was all in white—that dress with the fairy frills, you know—and had, what's more, A HEAD! At least, something white all wrapped around it, and over her shoulders. At first we thought you or some of the boys had dressed her up and lifted her out there for a joke, and left her to frighten us! So we started forward, and then—it's the gospel truth!—she MOVED AWAY, gliding like the moonbeams, and vanished among the trees!"

"Did you see her face?" asked the president.

"No; you bet! I didn't try to—it would have haunted me forever."

"What do you mean?"

"This—I mean it was that GIRL THE BOX BELONGED TO! She's dead somewhere—as you'll find out sooner or later—AND HAS COME BACK FOR HER CLOTHES! I've often heard of such things before."

Despite his coolness, at this corroboration of his own experience, and impressed by Grey's unmistakable awe, a thrill went through the president. For an instant he was silent.

"That will do, boys," he said finally. "It's a queer story; but remember, it's all the more reason now for our keeping our secret. As for those things, I'll remove them quietly and at once."

But he did not.

On the contrary, prolonging his stay at the hotel with plausible reasons, he managed to frequently visit the committee room or its vicinity, at different and unsuspected hours of the day and night. More than that, he found opportunities to visit the office, and under pretexts of business connected with the economy of the hotel management, informed himself through Miss Marsh on many points. A few of these details naturally happened to refer to herself, her prospects, her tastes, and education. He learned incidentally, what he had partly known, that her father had been in better circumstances, and that she had been gently nurtured—though of this she made little account in her pride in her own independence and devotion to her duties. But in his own persistent way he also made private notes of the breadth of her shoulders, the size of her waist, her height, length of her skirt, her movements in walking, and other apparently extraneous circumstances. It was natural that he acquired some supplemental facts,—that her eyes, under her eye-glasses, were a tender gray, and touched with the melancholy beauty of near-sightedness; that her face had a sensitive mobility beyond the mere charm of color, and like most people lacking this primitive and striking element of beauty, what was really fine about her escaped the first sight. As, for instance, it was only by bending over to examine her accounts that he found that her indistinctive hair was as delicate as floss silk and as electrical. It was only by finding her romping with the children of a guest one evening that he was startled by the appalling fact of her youth! But about this time he left the hotel and returned to his house.

On the first yearly anniversary of the great strike at Excelsior there were some changes in the settlement, notably the promotion of Mr. Marsh to a more important position in the company, and the installation of Miss Cassie Marsh as manageress of the hotel. As Miss Marsh read the official letter, signed by the president, conveying in complimentary but formal terms this testimony of their approval and confidence, her lip trembled slightly, and a tear trickling from her light lashes dimmed her eye-glasses, so that she was fain to go up to her room to recover herself alone. When she did so she was startled to find a wire dummy standing near the door, and neatly folded upon the bed two elegant dresses. A note in the president's own hand lay beside them. A swift blush stung her cheek as she read,—

DEAR MISS MARSH,—Will you make me happy by

keeping the secret that no other woman but yourself knows, and by accepting the clothes that no other woman but yourself can wear?

The next moment, with the dresses over her arm and the ridiculous dummy swinging by its wires from her other hand, she was flying down the staircase to Committee Room No. 4. The door opened upon its sole occupant, the president.

"Oh, sir, how cruel of you!" she gasped. "It was only a joke of mine. . . . I always intended to tell you. . . . It was very foolish, but it seemed so funny. . . . You see, I thought it was . . . the dress you had bought for your future intended—some young lady you were going to marry!"

"It is!" said the president quietly, and he closed the door behind her.

And it was.

ABOUT THE AUTHOR

 **Francis Bret Harte** (August 25, 1836–May 6, 1902) was an American author and poet, best remembered for his accounts of pioneering life in California.

Born in Albany, New York, Harte moved to California in 1853, later working there in a number of capacities, including miner, teacher, messenger, and journalist. He spent part of his life in the northern California coast town now known as Arcata, at the time it was just a mining camp on Humboldt Bay.

His first literary efforts, including poetry and prose, appeared in The Californian, an early literary journal edited by Charles Henry Webb. In 1868 he became editor of The Overland Monthly, another new literary magazine, but this one more in tune with the pioneering spirit of excitement in California. His story, "The Luck of Roaring Camp," appeared in the magazine's second edition, propelling Harte to nationwide fame.

As an established literary figure, he was appointed to the position of United States Consul in the town of Krefeld, Germany in 1878 and Glasgow in 1880. In 1885 he settled in London. During the thirty years he spent in Europe, he never abandoned writing, and maintained a prodigious output of stories that retained the freshness of his earlier work. He died in England in 1902.

Other books by this author

Maruja
Sally Dows and Other Stories
Stories in Light and Shadow
Tales of the Argonauts
Tales of Trail and Town
The Three Partners
Under the Redwoods
By Shore and Sedge
Colonel Starbottle's Client and Other Stories
Clarence
Cressy
Devil's Ford
Frontier Stories
In a Hollow of the Hills
In the Carquinez Woods
Jeff Briggs's Love Story
Snow-Bound at Eagle's
The Argonauts of North Liberty
The Bell-Ringer of Angel's and Other Stories
The Crusade of the Excelsior
The Story of a Mine

Choose from Thousands of 1stWorldLibrary Classics By

A. M. Barnard	Booth Tarkington	Edward Everett Hale
Ada Leverson	Boyd Cable	Edward J. O'Biren
Adolphus William Ward	Bram Stoker	Edward S. Ellis
Aesop	C. Collodi	Edwin L. Arnold
Agatha Christie	C. E. Orr	Eleanor Atkins
Alexander Aaronsohn	C. M. Ingleby	Eleanor Hallowell Abbott
Alexander Kielland	Carolyn Wells	Eliot Gregory
Alexandre Dumas	Catherine Parr Traill	Elizabeth Gaskell
Alfred Gatty	Charles A. Eastman	Elizabeth McCracken
Alfred Ollivant	Charles Amory Beach	Elizabeth Von Arnim
Alice Duer Miller	Charles Dickens	Ellem Key
Alice Turner Curtis	Charles Dudley Warner	Emerson Hough
Alice Dunbar	Charles Farrar Browne	Emilie F. Carlen
Allen Chapman	Charles Ives	Emily Bronte
Alleyne Ireland	Charles Kingsley	Emily Dickinson
Ambrose Bierce	Charles Klein	Enid Bagnold
Amelia E. Barr	Charles Hanson Towne	Enilor Macartney Lane
Amory H. Bradford	Charles Lathrop Pack	Erasmus W. Jones
Andrew Lang	Charles Romyn Dake	Ernie Howard Pie
Andrew McFarland Davis	Charles Whibley	Ethel May Dell
Andy Adams	Charles Willing Beale	Ethel Turner
Angela Brazil	Charlotte M. Braeme	Ethel Watts Mumford
Anna Alice Chapin	Charlotte M. Yonge	Eugene Sue
Anna Sewell	Charlotte Perkins Stetson	Eugenie Foa
Annie Besant	Clair W. Hayes	Eugene Wood
Annie Hamilton Donnell	Clarence Day Jr.	Eustace Hale Ball
Annie Payson Call	Clarence E. Mulford	Evelyn Everett-green
Annie Roe Carr	Clemence Housman	Everard Cotes
Annonaymous	Confucius	F. H. Cheley
Anton Chekhov	Coningsby Dawson	F. J. Cross
Archibald Lee Fletcher	Cornelis DeWitt Wilcox	F. Marion Crawford
Arnold Bennett	Cyril Burleigh	Fannie E. Newberry
Arthur C. Benson	D. H. Lawrence	Federick Austin Ogg
Arthur Conan Doyle	Daniel Defoe	Ferdinand Ossendowski
Arthur M. Winfield	David Garnett	Fergus Hume
Arthur Ransome	Dinah Craik	Florence A. Kilpatrick
Arthur Schnitzler	Don Carlos Janes	Fremont B. Deering
Arthur Train	Donald Keyhoe	Francis Bacon
Atticus	Dorothy Kilner	Francis Darwin
B.H. Baden-Powell	Dougan Clark	Frances Hodgson Burnett
B. M. Bower	Douglas Fairbanks	Frances Parkinson Keyes
B. C. Chatterjee	E. Nesbit	Frank Gee Patchin
Baroness Emmuska Orczy	E. P. Roe	Frank Harris
Baroness Orczy	E. Phillips Oppenheim	Frank Jewett Mather
Basil King	E. S. Brooks	Frank L. Packard
Bayard Taylor	Earl Barnes	Frank V. Webster
Ben Macomber	Edgar Rice Burroughs	Frederic Stewart Isham
Bertha Muzzy Bower	Edith Van Dyne	Frederick Trevor Hill
Bjornstjerne Bjornson	Edith Wharton	Frederick Winslow Taylor

Friedrich Kerst
Friedrich Nietzsche
Fyodor Dostoyevsky
G.A. Henty
G.K. Chesterton
Gabrielle E. Jackson
Garrett P. Serviss
Gaston Leroux
George A. Warren
George Ade
Geroge Bernard Shaw
George Cary Eggleston
George Durston
George Ebers
George Eliot
George Gissing
George MacDonald
George Meredith
George Orwell
George Sylvester Viereck
George Tucker
George W. Cable
George Wharton James
Gertrude Atherton
Gordon Casserly
Grace E. King
Grace Gallatin
Grace Greenwood
Grant Allen
Guillermo A. Sherwell
Gulielma Zollinger
Gustav Flaubert
H. A. Cody
H. B. Irving
H. C. Bailey
H. G. Wells
H. H. Munro
H. Irving Hancock
H. R. Naylor
H. Rider Haggard
H. W. C. Davis
Haldeman Julius
Hall Caine
Hamilton Wright Mabie
Hans Christian Andersen
Harold Avery
Harold McGrath
Harriet Beecher Stowe
Harry Castlemon
Harry Coghill
Harry Houidini

Hayden Carruth
Helent Hunt Jackson
Helen Nicolay
Hendrik Conscience
Hendy David Thoreau
Henri Barbusse
Henrik Ibsen
Henry Adams
Henry Ford
Henry Frost
Henry James
Henry Jones Ford
Henry Seton Merriman
Henry W Longfellow
Herbert A. Giles
Herbert Carter
Herbert N. Casson
Herman Hesse
Hildegard G. Frey
Homer
Honore De Balzac
Horace B. Day
Horace Walpole
Horatio Alger Jr.
Howard Pyle
Howard R. Garis
Hugh Lofting
Hugh Walpole
Humphry Ward
Ian Maclaren
Inez Haynes Gillmore
Irving Bacheller
Isabel Cecilia Williams
Isabel Hornibrook
Israel Abrahams
Ivan Turgenev
J. G.Austin
J. Henri Fabre
J. M. Barrie
J. M. Walsh
J. Macdonald Oxley
J. R. Miller
J. S. Fletcher
J. S. Knowles
J. Storer Clouston
J. W. Duffield
Jack London
Jacob Abbott
James Allen
James Andrews
James Baldwin

James Branch Cabell
James DeMille
James Joyce
James Lane Allen
James Lane Allen
James Oliver Curwood
James Oppenheim
James Otis
James R. Driscoll
Jane Abbott
Jane Austen
Jane L. Stewart
Janet Aldridge
Jens Peter Jacobsen
Jerome K. Jerome
Jessie Graham Flower
John Buchan
John Burroughs
John Cournos
John F. Kennedy
John Gay
John Glasworthy
John Habberton
John Joy Bell
John Kendrick Bangs
John Milton
John Philip Sousa
John Taintor Foote
Jonas Lauritz Idemil Lie
Jonathan Swift
Joseph A. Altsheler
Joseph Carey
Joseph Conrad
Joseph E. Badger Jr
Joseph Hergesheimer
Joseph Jacobs
Jules Vernes
Julian Hawthrone
Julie A Lippmann
Justin Huntly McCarthy
Kakuzo Okakura
Karle Wilson Baker
Kate Chopin
Kenneth Grahame
Kenneth McGaffey
Kate Langley Bosher
Kate Langley Bosher
Katherine Cecil Thurston
Katherine Stokes
L. A. Abbot
L. T. Meade

L. Frank Baum
Latta Griswold
Laura Dent Crane
Laura Lee Hope
Laurence Housman
Lawrence Beasley
Leo Tolstoy
Leonid Andreyev
Lewis Carroll
Lewis Sperry Chafer
Lilian Bell
Lloyd Osbourne
Louis Hughes
Louis Joseph Vance
Louis Tracy
Louisa May Alcott
Lucy Fitch Perkins
Lucy Maud Montgomery
Luther Benson
Lydia Miller Middleton
Lyndon Orr
M. Corvus
M. H. Adams
Margaret E. Sangster
Margret Howth
Margaret Vandercook
Margaret W. Hungerford
Margret Penrose
Maria Edgeworth
Maria Thompson Daviess
Mariano Azuela
Marion Polk Angellotti
Mark Overton
Mark Twain
Mary Austin
Mary Catherine Crowley
Mary Cole
Mary Hastings Bradley
Mary Roberts Rinehart
Mary Rowlandson
M. Wollstonecraft Shelley
Maud Lindsay
Max Beerbohm
Myra Kelly
Nathaniel Hawthrone
Nicolo Machiavelli
O. F. Walton
Oscar Wilde

Owen Johnson
P.G. Wodehouse
Paul and Mabel Thorne
Paul G. Tomlinson
Paul Severing
Percy Brebner
Percy Keese Fitzhugh
Peter B. Kyne
Plato
Quincy Allen
R. Derby Holmes
R. L. Stevenson
R. S. Ball
Rabindranath Tagore
Rahul Alvares
Ralph Bonehill
Ralph Henry Barbour
Ralph Victor
Ralph Waldo Emmerson
Rene Descartes
Ray Cummings
Rex Beach
Rex E. Beach
Richard Harding Davis
Richard Jefferies
Richard Le Gallienne
Robert Barr
Robert Frost
Robert Gordon Anderson
Robert L. Drake
Robert Lansing
Robert Lynd
Robert Michael Ballantyne
Robert W. Chambers
Rosa Nouchette Carey
Rudyard Kipling
Saint Augustine
Samuel B. Allison
Samuel Hopkins Adams
Sarah Bernhardt
Sarah C. Hallowell
Selma Lagerlof
Sherwood Anderson
Sigmund Freud
Standish O'Grady
Stanley Weyman
Stella Benson
Stella M. Francis

Stephen Crane
Stewart Edward White
Stijn Streuvels
Swami Abhedananda
Swami Parmananda
T. S. Ackland
T. S. Arthur
The Princess Der Ling
Thomas A. Janvier
Thomas A Kempis
Thomas Anderton
Thomas Bailey Aldrich
Thomas Bulfinch
Thomas De Quincey
Thomas Dixon
Thomas H. Huxley
Thomas Hardy
Thomas More
Thornton W. Burgess
U. S. Grant
Upton Sinclair
Valentine Williams
Various Authors
Vaughan Kester
Victor Appleton
Victor G. Durham
Victoria Cross
Virginia Woolf
Wadsworth Camp
Walter Camp
Walter Scott
Washington Irving
Wilbur Lawton
Wilkie Collins
Willa Cather
Willard F. Baker
William Dean Howells
William le Queux
W. Makepeace Thackeray
William W. Walter
William Shakespeare
Winston Churchill
Yei Theodora Ozaki
Yogi Ramacharaka
Young E. Allison
Zane Grey